AuthorHouse™
1663 Liberty Drive
Bloomington, IN 47403
www.authorhouse.com
Phone: 833-262-8899

Published by AuthorHouse 12/01/2021

ISBN: 978-1-6655-4627-0 (sc)
ISBN: 978-1-6655-4635-5 (e)

Library of Congress Control Number: 2021924884

Print information available on the last page.

It was a cold night in Portland Oregon for young Shay and Nikki. They were getting dressed for a party called the spring bling at a bar called (kings wild) and everybody who was somebody was going to be there. Nikki who is Shay's cousin really didn't want to go to the club tonight but Shacoyia (aka) Coyia bugged her to go cause she didn't want to go alone tonight, just in case some bitches started tripping and wanted to gang up on her cause they was too scared to catch the fade alone with her like real boss bitches do. Coyia had on some red pumps that stood 10 inch off the ground and that also made her a lot taller than what she really was. She wore a black mini skirt that hung over her ass, so her special someone could get a real good feel and maybe she could meet her knight and shining armor tonight.

She had on a red in black skirt that matches everything she had on, and it was outlined with white stitching that went with her earrings. That was a gift from her favorite cousin Nikki. Her hair was flat ironed and braided in a design on one side of her head like the R&B singer (Alicia keys) As for her cousin Nikki she just threw on some white jeans and a black shirt with the letters {like me or love me, your choice} written on her shirt. She had her hair pulled back in a ponytail and she just threw on her retro Jordan sneakers. Shay said "Damn bitch why you look so damn plain." Nikki responded "because bitch, I got a man at home and

I'm representing him at all times, bitch, why you look so damn ratchet all the time." Coyia smiled and said "Cause I'm looking for my black knight to come swoop me off my feet tonight and for us to start our crazy special life together, that's why bitch!" Nikki thought to herself not dressed like that you aint, but if you like it I love it. Shay replied "And I love looking like this" Nikki just rolled her eyes and they kept on getting dressed and Shay did the same thing. They finished up with their finishing touches and headed out the door to the party.

When they arrived the place was packed. "It's cracking up here tonight, damn the line is around the corner bitch." They saw people outside popping it, bitches were shaking their asses yelling "fuck the club, shit the clubs right here!" {repeatedly} There weren't any parking spots so they had to park around the corner. Coyia said "fuck that, I'm parking at the bar next door, so we don't have to walk to far, I got my handicap sticker, Nikki just laugh. Nikki said to Coyia "Bitch how the fuck are we going to get in here tonight, bitch I aint waiting in that long ass line, fuck that?" As they walked past everyone standing in line, Nikki happened to see the security was a friend she went to college with. Nikki yelled his name "Lamarcus, fatboy." she got louder as they walked faster towards him "P rock!" Then he turned around to see sexy ass Nikki, even without being dressed to impress she was still bomb as hell. P rock said "Nikki, Nikki, Nikki damn baby girl, long time no see." Nikki just smiled and said "I know, how you been doing?" P rock said "good, shit better than most." Nikki said "I see you doing big things Mr. Security officer." They both laughed and Coyia did as well, but she was getting restless with all the chit chatting and small talk. Coyia said in a sweet but demanding voice "Well since you Mr. big security officer can you get us in the club cause my feet hurt and I don't think it can last much longer standing here, I need these babies to help me drop it like it hot when I'm in there and being in that line ain't going to help me do that." Nikki smiled and said "do what," Coyia turned around and dropped her ass all the way to the ground and back up to a standing

2

position as she swung her hair and snapped her fingers while turning towards P rock and said "Help me drop it like it hot."

P rock looked her up and down and said "No doubt lil' mama, come on." They followed P rock into the building. When they walked inside it was cracking, you saw stripers on poles swinging and twisting and doing all kinds of flips. Their asses were shaking at lightning speeds as if they were a washing machines. You seen niggas popping at bitches from wall to wall and flashing their money and letting it rain all over the bitches in the club. you saw all the hood bitches that were about something and the ratchet bitches that were looking for a baller to leave with. You seen bitches drunk ass fuck in there showing they asses and acting a fool. Coyia and Nikki looked to the left and to the right and saw security breaking up fights left and right. Ahead of them people were shooting pool and behind them they saw the poker machines were full with a line behind it. "It's packed in this bitch, damn," Nikki shook her head and said "hell yeah". The security had to run off on them to help break up some of the fights. Nikki said "it's hot in here, let's go to the back so I can smoke, I ain't trying to sweat out my perm already," Coyia said "shit I can't wait to sweat this shit out, and somebody gone be pulling my hair by the end of night. Nikki just shook her head as they made their way to the back so Nikki could smoke a cigarette. Coyia walked out the door first and saw her coworker Amber was facing the door and saw Coyia as well. Coyia smiled and yelled "Amber"!!!! Amber ran into Coyia arms and they hugged each other like they ain't seen each other in years. Nikki said "yall act like yall didn't just get off work together a couple of hours ago". They both cracked up because they knew she was right. Nikki walked to the table and sat down by two empty chairs to smoke her cigarette. Amber asked Coyia "when yall get here"? Coyia said we just walked in this bitch, how long have you been here"? Amber said a couple of hours it's been cracking since I got here," Coyia said "I see the line is all the way around the corner."

Amber was a white girl that was hood. She was raised by black folks or should I say hood people cause her mom was just as ghetto but she died from cancer and her best friend took Amber in and raised her as their own. Amber was ghetto though as ghetto as they came. From cooking to doing hair to fighting, that bitch done it all, her only problem was that she loved some good dick and could tell you everybody's business because she fucked with everyone's man, but that was Coyia's bitches cause Coyia could relate to her and that had their drunken days and ratchet times together. Amber asked Coyia "You see that black sexy thing over there" Coyia looked at all the guys around her and said "I see them", Amber said "No bitch, not them," Amber grabbed Coyia showers and spun her around and pointed "right there bitch"? Coyia said "Oh, Jesus there is a god, you see that one with the dreads" Amber said "hell yea and that Armani suit is on point too". Coyia stare at the man Amber showed her and get wet between her legs thinking about how she would ride the fuck out of him. Nikki walked over to her girls and looked in the direction they were looking and said "yall staring at them niggas over there, and why the fuck is he wearing a three-piece suit at a bar". Coyia said "I don't know, but he's fine as hell" Nikki shook her head and said if you say so" and laughed. Coyia said "I hope he ain't a pimp, Amber you should go see if he's a pimp or not" Amber said "Why I always have to see about shit" Coyia said because you always the one to point niggas out and you the boldest one out of me in you and this bitch is married and you know she won't do it" Nikki said you damn right I can't wait to get home to my husband, shit let me go call him right now why we talking about him," and she walked off with her phone in her hand. Nikki said will since you scared to go over there I'ma claiming the one with the dreads" Coyia said naw it's a fair game cause what if he don't want you, and starts talking to me" Amber said "Will bold I am and I don't give a fuck about him being a pimp, cause he ain't pimpin me, and he better have some money cause that's all I want and that big chocolate dick between his legs". They laughed and Amber started walking towards the men.

As she got halfway to the men, the one with the dreads tapped his friend on the shoulder and said "man hear comes this ghetto as bitch man y'all have fun, I want the one she was talking to, now watch what I do come on bro let's do it how we us to do back in the day" his home boy dress and to her surprise the dread headed homie boy jumped right in front of her and said "How you doing my name young fate", the dread headed guy walked right past Amber without looking in her direction, but said excuse me when he passed her. The dread headed man walked right to Coyia and held his hand out and said "How are you doing? My name is melo." Coyia looked over his shoulder and looked at Amber. Amber stood looking at both of them and seen Coyia look at her, Amber stomped her feet and said to herself "Fuck it, we both got one", and kept it pushing with the one that started talking to her. Melo looked back with a grin on his face only to see Amber smiling at him or Coyia while shaking her head. Melo thought to himself "Yea bitch you got played". but it didn't look like she was trippin because she walked off with hit home boy fate. Coyia was in a daze staring at Melo, and you could see sex in her eyes the way she stared at him. she looked down only to see Melo's hand extended out to her. Coyia said "Ooooo huh", "my name is Melo and yours is"? Coyia shook melo's hand and said "You're hopefully" they both laughed and she said "nah I'm playing, but my name is Coyia" At that moment Coyia told herself that he was going to be her man. When Nikki got back to the table she was sitting at. She looked around for her friends and decided to call her husband again to see what he was doing and to check on the kids. Nikki was happy to have something to live for, a family of her own.

Melo and Coyia talked for a while and got to know each other a little better. When the crowd started going in, Coyia heard her song inside the club and asked melo to dance. He agreed and they went inside to get their party on together. As soon as they walked inside melo instantly started doing the stanky leg. Coyia started cracking up cause seeing melo do the stanky in a three piece was a sight to see. Coyia said "That suit looks a little tight on you right now", and they both cracked up. Melo said to Coyia "I thought you said this was supposed to be your favorite song, why aint see you do nothing yet," Coyia started doing the stanky leg and killed it.

People looked and saw a cute couple dancing. Coyia got tired of dancing in front of Melo so she turned around and put her ass against him and made sure that she could feel his dick through his pants. She pushed up against him hard and seductively. Melo knew she was sizing him up because she kept grinding hard against him, so he grabbed the side of her hips and pushed into her hard. Coyia turned her head and looked at him to let him know she knew what he was doing. Melo already had a smile on his face and started rubbing her thighs to let her know that he was with the business. After drinking and dancing for hours in Coyia walked off the dance floor and told Nikki and Amber that she was going with Melo and that she didn't need a ride home. Coyia and Amber hugged and Amber started laughing saying "shit, I'm going with his homeboy tonight too". They both laughed and clapped hands. Nikki looked at both of them and said "y'all bitches is some nasty hoes and both of yall gonna catch something," they all laughed but Nikki was serious about what she had said, all they do is fuck all kinds of guy's as soon as they meet them and nikki couldn't stand that. In her mind there was really no point in coming with coyia because she always did the same thing every time they went out. Coyia said will this is about to be my nigga so if he got something, then we got something together and Amber said will when I find someone and if he has something I swear to God he gon die if he try to leave me with any STD. They all started laughing again. Nikki said (look y'all ain't going to find Mr. right in no club and especially if y'all keep fucking these mothafucka's as soon as y'all meet them.) Coyia said (I will), and shook Amber's hand and they all hugged and departed their own ways. As they made it out the parking lot Melo was parked in front and Coyia jumped inside his car. Nikki got outside with a pin and a piece of paper and she was looking at the car and writing something down, then she walked right up to Melo's car and said (rolled down the window) he did as he was asked. Coyia said (o my god, what now?) Nikki said (shut up) and looked Melo in his eyes and said (look this is my cousin, and my favorite cousin at that, so she better make it home tomorrow or we gon have problems) and she showed Melo the piece of paper with his license plate numbers on it. Melo just laughed and said (don't worry pretty lady, she's in good hands) Nikki said that's good to know cause if I don't hear from her in the morning, I'll be there early in the morning with my 9mm and my husband 45 in both hands ready to look for yo ass. You got me.

Coyia yelled and cut her off "damn okay bitch, can we leave now mama. "We're going to my house so you know i'll be cool, now bye bitch". Nikki smiled back and said can I get your name again? He reached out his hand and said Melo and your name is? I'm Nikki the bitch you shouldn't fuck with and nice to meet you and y'all be safe tonight and i'll call you tomorrow morning bitch so answer the phone when i call. They drove off as she walked yelling at them. She kept her eyes on the car as they drove away. Coyia and Melo had small talk on the way to Coyia's house and Coyia couldn't wait until they got there. As soon as Melo walked into Coyia's house he was stunned at all the sexual artifacts in her living room. Melo said, damn, either you a freak and love to fuck or just a person that loves sex artifacts." Coyia laughed and responded "you wanna find out," and started walking toward Melo. Melo said "hell yea" and as soon as Coyia got to him they started kissing and grabbing and touching and rubbing each other. He grabbed her ass tightly and lifted her up and turned her around. Coyia grabbed his hands and put them on her breast as Melo kissed and sucked on her neck. He grabbed her hair and a seductive way and put her hair into a ponytail and pulled her head back towards him roughly but not to much to fuck up the mode up. Dick harder than a baseball bat ready to play ball. Coyia played with herself as she grinded on his dick with her ass. Coyia felt a warm sensation building up between her thighs and a rush of pleasure going through her body at the same time. She moaned loudly and her body twisted from side to side as she came on her own. Melo got harder and harder with the sounds that Coyia was making and he couldn't take it anymore, he put his hand in between her thighs and started playing with her with one hand and pulling her hair with the other. Coyia was in pure bliss as Mele played with her and she was ready to come again. Coyia took his fingers and put them on her clitorous and started squirting as she arched her back deep into Melo's dick. Coyia couldn't take the foreplay anymore, so she pulled his hand out of her and turned to him and dropped to her knees and started sucking his dick. Melo just stood there and rolled his head back as she sucked his dick for dear life.

He grabbed the back of her head with both hands and was about to cum and he pulled out. Coyia said "fuck that, I'm running the show right now, take yo ass over there and sit on that couch no"!) Melo just smiled and did as he was told. He started to unbutton his pants and Coyia said "Did I say you could do that," he just laughed and sat there while Coyia walked to him slowly and seductively. Coyia dropped to her knees and said "you're my king and this is always going to be yours". Melo just smiled and let her undo his pants. Coyia thought to herself "why not get used to doing this everyday", and she dug right in. Coyia sucked Melo dick like no other could. she spits on it, kissed it, licked it, even moaned on it, she even stuffed it deep in her mouth and tried to go as far as she could to her stomach without throwing up on her new man's dick. Melo just sat back and enjoyed the bomb as head he was getting. He thought to himself "fuck it's late, I need to get home before wifey starts tripping and starts blowing me up, I need to speed up this process before shit hits the fan." Melo pulled Coyia up and hiked up her skirt and said "come on". Coyia got up and pulled her panties down and started getting on top, but Melo put his hands on her hips and said "whoa, slow down baby, let me get a rubber real quick." Coyia felt kind of embarrassed, she aint met to many dudes that stopped in the middle of sex to put on a rubber, but she understood that they had just met and he has to get use to her. Coyia thought to herself

"Shit, don't get use to that daddy, I want the real deal, and I need all your babies inside me because your mine now." Melo grabbed a condom out his wallet and slipped it on his dick. Coyia played with herself while he slipped it on. Melo said "come on mama let's do this baby" and Coyia followed his command and climbed on top of him. Her goal was to make Melo wiped and she went to acting school. she bounced on his dick and grinded it. She would go all the way to the tip of his dick and push it inside of her as far as it could go. when she would start to cum she would grind on his dick long and hard so they both felt wetness on each other. Melo was surprised that Coyia could take all his dick the way she was, normally most girls would only go inside halfway cause his dick was so big, but not Coyia she acted like his dick wasn't shit and that turned Melo on and that made him want to hit it from the back doggy style.

As Coyia rode Melo to no return she couldn't stop thinking about how big his dick was. It was tearing up her stomach but the pleasure that she got from that and the nuts she kept having kept her on top and she came hard on that dick. Melo looked at his watch to see the time and he knew he had to be getting home soon, but he didn't want to stop because Coyia was riding the shit out of him and she took it all, something that his wife couldn't do and that kept him there but, he was a family man and kept his business in the street and never let the streets come before home so he had to make an audible. He told Coyia to get up so he could hit it from the back. Coyia stood up and Melo followed suit. She bent over and held onto the living room table and Melo put his dick inside of Coyia while pulling her hair and thrusting inside of her. Melo stood on his tiptoes and tightened all his muscles in his body. He concentrated on nutting and thought about the nasty shit he and his wife do in the privacy of their home. Different sensation started to flow though his body and his leg started to shake and he grabbed Coyia's hip and beat the dog shit out of her pussy. Coyia screamed loudly cause she had never came so hard before, her body shook and her legs couldn't stand much longer. Her eyes

Devon Campbell-Williams

rolled to the back of her head as she broke her nails trying to squeezes the table. Melo felted what he had come for, and he knew it was a big one. He started slowing down but kept hitting it hard with nice strokes until he nutted and it shot out of him, he fell on Coyia and she fell to the floor, on their way to the floor he kept pumping and nothing but pure ecstasy flowed through both of these bodies, as he laid on top of her and Coyia laid on the floor with her ass hicked in the air. She didn't know he was about to nut, but she sure was happy cause her stomach killed her and he legs couldn't stand any longer.

Coyia rolled to the side so he could get off her and Coyia started wiping away the sweat that was running down his face. Melo said to Coyia while he was breathing heavily "can you go turn on the shower and bring me something to drink." Coyia said "give me a second baby, let me catch my breath real quick", they both laid there trying to catch the breath. Coyia got up and went into the kitchen and brought Melo a bottle of ice cold water. Melo down the water and coyia said "let me get my stuff together ima get in the shower with you." Melo shook his head and a yes motion and started getting up off the floor Coyia walked off to turn on the water and the bathroom. Then walked into her room to grab her clothes to wear after they showered. Coyia whole plan was to take a shower with Melo and go cook him some food while they watched movies and went to bed, but that all changed when Coyia heard the front door closes. Coyia walked out to the hallway and yelled "is somebody at the door Melo ", but Coyia didn't get a response. She said his name again (Melo) as she walked into the living room only to see no one sitting on her couch. Coyia walked around her house looking for him then she went to the front door to make sure he wasn't smoking a cigarette. She opened the door and didn't see him or his car in front of her house and that fucked Coyia up. Coyia's heart felt like it went from her chest to her throat and tears fell from her face. She closed the door and slid down the wall because her prince charming had left. Not only did he leave, but he did it so cowardly and that hurt because she really

10

put it on him and really wanted him to be hers. It hurt and it hurt Coyia badly. All she did that night was cry. The next day Coyia's cousin Nikki called to check on her, but got no answer. She called a few times just to see if she was sleeping hard, because she knew she had gotten dicked down last night. She just didn't want anything bad to happen to her favorite cousin.

So Nikki decided to go to her house to check on her favorite cousin, but before she left she left a message on Coyia's answering machine. "Bitch, if you don't answer this mothafucking phone, I'm coming over there and kick the door down, matter a fact, ima use that key you gave me, and that **SEXY MOTHAFUCKA YOU WITH BET NOT BE NAKED EITHER OR IM GOING HAM, SO COVER HIS SEXY CHOCOLATE DROPPED ASS UP**"!! Nikki's husband heard his wife saying she was about to go to Coyia's house and said "NO THE FUCK YOU AIN'T GOING NOWHERE!" Nikki thought he heard her say she was going to see a naked man at Coyia house. Nikki turned around in fear and said "huh" and a hesitant voice. Nikki's husband was walking toward her and she almost dropped the phone out of fear. He got to her and said "what did you say", Nikki didn't say anything. He said "fuck that you owe me for watching the kids last night remember, I need mine before you do anything or go anywhere, I sat here all night with these kids crying screaming and hollering and im horny, you promise me you would suck my dick before you left and you forgot, then when we talked on the phone last night and you swore if you came in and I was sleep you would wake me up to some bomb as head now I ask you and demand your ass to suck this dick," (with a big smile on his face). Nikki smiled and felt relief go through her body. She told Coyia's answering machine "bitch yall better be covered up when I get there, and his dick bet not be little either." Nikki said that as quietly as she could because her husband was standing behind her stroking his dick while staring at her and backing towards the couch. Nikki started pulling down her sweats and said "bye bitch, I'll be there after I'm done here and Nikki hung the phone up and kept her word to her husband and had a big smile on her face while she did it too. Coyia woke up to an empty bed and was bummed that she slept alone without prince charming next to her. She heard her phone ringing but didn't feel like answering it. Coyia heard her phone ring again and when her answering machine came on it was her cousin Nikki on the other line leaving a message. Coyia cried because she heard her cousin's husband talking on the other side of the phone and that's all Coyia wanted. She wanted someone to wake up to. To be held when times got rough. Someone to tell her she was beautiful when she knew she was looking rough that day. She just wanted a family and would do whatever she had to do to get it. Coyia laid in her dark room with the windows closed and the T.V. off, She just wanted someone she could go on double dates with Nikki and her man. Just thinking about that made her cry harder. Coyia turned on the t.v and started flipping through the channels to find something to take her mind off of having a man. She dropped the remote and said (fuck it I'll just watch whatever is on this channel, and she laid her head on her pillow and watched commercials until a movie comes on. By the time something came on Coyia was asleep again.

Coyia woke up to Nikki standing over her yelling her name "Shacoyia, Shacoyia, bitch you hear me talking to you, I don't know why you acting slee", Coyia rolled over and said "What, Shit, Fucking leave me alone, damn", and Coyia through the covers over her head. Nikki knew something was wrong and sat on the bed and slowly pulled the cover off Coyia's head and said to coyia in a motherly voice "tell me what happened baby," Coyia insteadly started crying and sat up to hug Nikki. Coyia said "man, why do niggas always do me bad, I mean it ain't like I have a disease or something and I ain't looking to be married right now, but why me, why do I always have to get the short in of the stick, what is it about me that makes men run away or even do me like this period," Nikki said and a motherly voice while holding Coyia tight "nothing baby, nothing at all, it's them, that's all it is, we gon find you a good man one day, one with good credit and a car and his own place, it's just going to take some time, that's all." Coyia cried out louder and cried "Why can't I find someone like what you got, that only wants me for me and treats me how your man does you," Nikki just held Coyia closes and told her he was out there and that she would find him one day, but she just had to be patient that's all. Nikki said "Don't sweat it we gonna find you a goddess too," They both laughed and Coyia said "you stupid girl", Nikki said "shit I aint playing, shit fuck that, we going to the club tonight to see if he's there tonight too". They busted into laughter. Coyia agreed with her cousin and said "you right girl, that's his loss, fuck that nigga, he's missing out," Nikki replied "okay", and they hugged each other tightly. While they were still hugging Nikki happened to look at the T.V. to see what Coyia was watching. Nikki said "ooooooooooo, shit this is that movie called (misery) **Girl** this is a bomb as movie, That white lady is crazier than a mothafucka," "have you seen this movie."

Coyia replied "naw it was just on when I got up, shit you came in while I was sleep bitch remember, but what is it about?" Nikki slapped her hands together and started explaining all dramatically to Coyia about the movie. "Girl it's about this white lady that saves this white dude who was an author and kidnaps him at the same time. This white girl broke his legs and just torchers him". "Bitch, this shit will have you going crazy in this mothafucka", Coyia just smiled and said "it sounds like a damn good movie, shit the way you all dramatic and shit, but how far am I into this movie already." Nikki looked at the TV and said "it looks like it's about over." Nikki said "fuck all this dark shit, bitch open a curtain and this bitch, damn this shit ain't the business bitch, and get dressed so we can go eat I'm hungry." Coyia got up and jumped in the shower then got dressed.

As they drove down the street in Nikki's car, they were thinking about where they were going to eat. Nikki asked "Where we eating at sexy lady", Coyia replied "I don't know", Nikki looked over and said "Sexy lady you looking good bitch", Coyia smiled and said "thank you", Nikki only said that because she knew Coyia was still hurting about last night, and she just wanted to make her cousin smile. Nikki asked Coyia "Do you want to go to that place on 42 and killingsworth, ain't it called Mr. Burger, or star burgers or something like that." Coyia laughed and said "bitch you mean Mr. Burger, but I ain't been there in a long time," Nikki said "for real tho, you trying to go there then?" Coyia said "I don't care." They headed in that direction. When they got there the place was closed down and Nikki was mad, "Fuck I'm hungry as fuck, shit"!

Coyia said "let's just go to that chicken place on 9th and alberta, then, in get some of that crack chicken", Nikki smiled and said "hell yeah, and the food is ready to, so I don't have to wait either." Nikki sped up to go to 9th and alberta for some chicken. They pulled up to 9th and lberta and Nikki got mad instead, "now I know why I don't come here again, fuck there ain't never no parking around this bitch." Coyia just laughed and sat up to help Nikki look for a parking spot. Nikki saw a spot across the street and parked across the street on the other side of Alberta. Coyia yelled "bitch you know your next to a fire hydrant," Nikki said "I don't give a fuck about all that, we aint going to be in there that long anyways, come on." They both cracked up and got out and headed to the store. The city bus pulled up to the bus stop right in front of the store and people started getting off. Coyia and Nikki walked right in front of the bus while it was letting people get off. Coyia reached for the door and someone yelled her name as she opened the door to the store, (Coyia).

She turned to see her old friend Ant from high school with his smirk on his face. He said "what's happening mama", with his arms out. Coyia just laughed and ran to him and gave him a big hug. "Ant what the fuck are you doing over here, I ain't seen you in a long time, how you been doing"? Ant hugged Coyia tightly and spun her around in the air, and said "what's good little mama, and I been good, what about yourself", Coyia said "good now that I've seen you," Ant said "is that right, will you know I always wanted yo sexy ass anyways," Coyia stomach had butterflies swarming all around in it and she just blushed cause she felt the same way and on top of that her dad always called her sexy lady and that made her feel special. At that moment Coyia felt herself getting wet between her legs just by his words he was saying to her and the tank top that he had showed all of his cuts and muscles and Coyia was feening for attention from anyone at this moment in her life especially since Melo pulled that shit last night.

Coyia had flashbacks about Ant and her nipples got hard just by staring at him. Ant was 5'9 with a dark complexion skin, and a hair that any woman would die for, on top of that it was tapered on the sides and in the back of his head and. That made Coyia want him just as bad now than before. Coyia said "shit about to go get some of this crack chicken, you stay around here," Ant said "naw, I just got off the bus to grab me a beer real quick then go to my cousins house". Coyia said "coo, then can we go into the store together then". They walk into the store together laughing and Coyia sees Nikki at the front counter already paying for her food. Ant walked back to the beer section to grab him a beer and headed to Coyia by Nikki at the front counter. Coyia kept looking at Ant as he went to the back to grab his beer and when he started walking back to her she thought to herself (what if it's Ant that supposed to be my black knight, I mean Nikki did say I was going to meet me a man tonight, I mean it ain't night but shit its close enough.) Coyia smiled and said to "Ant, what are you getting into tonight," he smiled and said "shit, hopefully kicking it with you." Coyia smiled and said "will okay, I didn't feel like going to the club tonight anyways so we have a date", Ant smiled and said to her "give me your phone and if your serious you'll hit me when you want me to come though", Coyia gave him her phone and he put his number in her phone as well. Coyia said "trust, I'm serious so don't play", and they both laughed and gave each other a hug and walked off. Coyia stopped right before she walked out the store and turned around and asked Ant what he wanted to eat, Ant looked at Coyia and said "fried chicken, or pork chops, better yet surprise me with something".

He walked up to Coyia and reached out and grabbed the door and held it for her to walk out. Coyia stood their puzzle and just stared at him, Ant blew her a kiss and walked off. Coyia walked out the store with a smile on her face and rushed to the car. She was ready to get home to unthaw that meat she had in the freezer. As soon as she got to the car Nikki said with a stuffed mouth and greasy face "bitch, what took you so long, I'm on my last piece of chicken and I'm about ready to start on yours". Coyia with the biggest smile said "I got a date tonight, so take me home so I can unthaw this meat and get ready for tonight. Nikki said to Coyia "okay bitch don't let it be another run away, and remember you don't have to open your legs for a man to want you". Coyia said "naw, not two in a row, and I know him, he ain't like that. I went to school with him and he was never like that". There was silence in the car on the way back to Coyia house.

When Coyia got home, she ran straight to the kitchen to find some food for Ant to eat. She knew everything was frozen so she took everything out to find some chicken. When she found it, she put everything back in the freezer and put the chicken in some cold water to thaw out. She talked to herself while she did everything. She went to the bedroom and straightened her room up and made sure nothing was on the floor and she made sure she changed the bedding from last night.

After she finished that she went into the living room and made sure that there was on signs of Melo being there. She fluffed out the pillows and made sure there was nothing that was on the couch or in between the couch. Coyia opened the windows and aired out her house just in case there was a smell or a stinch lingering around.

Coyia vacuumed the floors and cleaned up the bathroom as well. When she finished cleaning the bathroom she went and shut the windows and doors and lit some incense and went to see if the chicken was thawed out enough to cook. She talked to herself again and said to herself "I wonder if ribs would be cool for him, naw, what about frys", she shook her head and just left it with what she loved best, chicken macaroni and veggies. While she was grabbing everything to cook, she started daydreaming of rubbing

Ant's body with ice cubes and kissing his muscles with the ice cubes and slowly making her way to his stomach one ab at a time. Coyia started getting a warm sensation between her legs, and she crossed her legs and put one hand between her legs and the other on her breast with the frozen veggies. She must have been daydreaming hard because she dropped the veggies on the floor and that snapped her out of whatever trend she was in. Coyia said to herself "I need to get into the bath because I'm hornier than a mothafucka". Coyia bit her bottom lip and shook her head and smiled and said "I feel nasty as shit for fucking somebody last night and now im thinking about fucking a different person tonight". I'm just going to kick it tonight, no fucking involved like nikki said. So let me go get my nut out the way now, and she went into the bathroom to start the bath. She went into the bedroom to grab her handy friend BOB aka her (DILDO) and while she was grabbing it out the drawer next to her bed, the phone rang. Coyia answered the phone and to her surprise it was Ant. He said "what's good lil mama, we still on for tonight", Coyia said yea, i was just about to call you, I'm cooking right after I get out the shower", he asked "what are you cooking tonight sexy lady", Coyia smiled because her dad use to call her that Coyia said "I'm glad you called because i'm looking in the freezer right now and I can't decide if you would want chicken or ribs, but I thawed the chicken but I don't think the ribs would be done by the time you got here". Ant said fuck that, I need that shit done by the time I get there so just cook the chicken and it better be good too", they both laughed. Ant told her that he would be there in two hours, coyia smiled and said "okay see you when you get here".They hung up the phone and Coyia through the phone on the couch and ran and cut the water off and got into the bath to please herself before Ant got there.

Coyia handled her business in the bath and got up to take a quick shower then jumped out to start cooking. Coyia cooked everything to perfection, she didn't want anything to go wrong and didn't want to make something too salty or without enough salt. So she took her time. It was too quiet in the house so she went into the living room and turned on her favorite cd by her favorite r&b singer (**Lyfe Jennings**) the first song was (must be nice). What made Coyia feel good about herself was that it really felt nice to cook for someone other than herself and she danced and cooked while singing to the smooth groove she was playing. Coyia thought to herself "I'ma cook more than enough just in case he wants more or he wants to take some home when he leaves". When everything was done she smelled her clothes and they smelt like chicken. she said out loud to herself "I know this boy wanted chicken, but why do I gotta smell like it too"?

She laughed to herself and she decided to take another shower and to put on some of her secret lingerie that she had been saving for a rainy day. See through panties that were red with black outlining and a matching bra set with a beautiful red dress that had a slit in the left side going toward the right side of her right thigh, but stopped right before her secret place. When she got done putting on her clothes, she lotioned up and put on some of her expensive perfume from Victoria's Secret. As Coyia started looking at herself in the mirror. She noticed the dress fit against her body perfectly. It showed all her curves and set her breast up perfectly. She put on a nice diamond necklace with matching earrings. She put on her heels that match her earrings and dress and talked to herself about how the night was going to go. She said to herself (take it slow, he's not like Melo from, you know him from high school and he aint like these other men out here, but just take it slow and no fucking tonight, tonight is only about catching up and having fun.) She applied the finishing touches to her make-up and the doorbell rang. Coyia said to herself "just in time", and blew herself a kiss and went to open the door. As she started getting closer to the front door, she heard two people on the other side of the door and that made her stomach bubble. She felt butterflies swarming all around her stomach and she got curious on who was at her door. She said to herself (I know this nigga aint got no one with him,) and she opened the door only to see Ant and another guy talking. Coyia looked at Ant and he walked up to her, kissed her on the cheek and walked inside the house while saying to her "Damn, you sexier than a mouthafucka baby"! Coyia just looked at him and watched him walk inside her house. The other guy called her name (Shacoyia). She turned around slowly and looked at him. He said "you don't remember me now"? Coyia was puzzled for a second, then he spoke again, "it me lil chingy, Ant brother, the one that always used to throw water at you and your home girls at the park and yall used to chase me all around the park". Coyia started laughing and said "lil chingy" and she went in for a hug. He said "yea, you better not have forgotten about me, and don't call me that, anymore, it's just rell now". Coyia said "my bad rell, but you're always going to be lil chingy to me". They laughed and Coyia said "what are you doing here, this is supposed to be a date"? Rell said "will I was at the house and didn't have nothing to do, so i asked ant if it was okay to come over to see you, and big bro told me to asked you, and I asked him if it was okay to come and eat since you were cooking, and he said it was up to you, but I know I should've have called first but I knew yall were having a dinner date and a brother skinning as fuck, but this is you guys night and I swear, yall won't even know I was here if you let me stay, please Coyia"?

Coyia just laughed and said "will I guess you can come in, but remember this is a date, so go make a plate and go into my room and you better not touch anything, cause i'll be in there to check on you," tarell said "deal".

When they walked into the house they saw Ant's mouth was full of food and he was stuffing more food in his mouth. Rell said "damn slow your fat ass down boy, ain't nobody going to take your food from you". Ant almost choked and they all busted out laughing. Rell walked into the kitchen and washed his hands and asked Coyia where her room was after make his plate, she said "down the hall to the right and don't be going through my stuff either", he said "I won't dang", and walked down the hall to Coyia's room. When he got into her room he could tell she was doing her make-up because it was all over her dresser out of place.

He grabbed the remote controller off the bed and turned on the TV and flipped through the channels to find something to watch while he ate his meal. Ant was just finishing his food when Coyia got to the dinner table. Coyia prayed over her food and when she finished praying she got up from the table and went to her stereo system and turned on some music while they ate. Ant got loud and said "AWWWWW SHIT, that's my jam right there girl, what you know about that baby making music, huh", Coyia put on **(without you by Latif.)** She said "what you trying to say, because ain't no babies being made in here tonight", they both started laughed.

Ant got up from his chair and walked up to Coyia with his hand out and a beer that he brought in the other hand. He asked Coyia for a dance, and she accepted his offer. They danced together in a slow romantic mode. Ant had one hand around her waist and the other on his bottle of beer. Coyia melted in his arms and she loved how it felt being in them. The night was almost perfect, except for that nasty ass malt liquor he had been drinking on since he came in. That shit stank every time he tried to whisper something in her ear, "you should turn the lights down and light some candles to better our mode". Coyia saw where this was going. So she did as she was asked and turned the lights down and lit some of her new scented candles that she was waiting to lit, and some of her incense she had as well. On her way back to him, he asked "You ain't got no drank to better the mode"? Coyia went into the kitchen and grabbed a bottle of gin she had for rainy days and she grabbed a couple of glasses out of the covert and walked to the living room table. She told him to hold on because she had to grab some juice out of the refrigerator because she hated how gin tasted. When she came back Ant was pouring himself a shot and throwing them back. Coyia gave them some strong shots and Ant had to use the bathroom out the blue. Coyia took that time to catch up to his level. She threw three shots down as fast as she could and boy did it burn going down her throat.

When she heard the toilet flush she downed two more shots. When Ant came out of the bathroom Coyia felt her buzz coming on. When he got back to her he looked at the bottle and saw she drank most of it he said "Damn, you drank most of the bottle, was you trying to catch up to me or something", Coyia just laughed and shocked her head and a yes movement. She made them another shot and Ant told her to come dance again. Coyia tried to get up and almost fell over, she saved herself by holding on to the table. Ant tried to reach for her and she pushed his hand away and said "I got it, move i aint drunk ". Ant laughed because he knew she was drunk and about to be on a good one tonight. All he was thinking about was fucking her pussy up tonight. All he kept telling himself was (I'm fucking tonight), with a big grin on his face. Coyia made it back into Ant's arms and it seemed like his hands went straight for her ass. Coyia didn't mind it too much because they were dancing, but she had a grin on her face as well. So Coyia pushed herself into him. Ant danced well and Coyia closed her eyes and thought about her life that she could be having with Ant. The alcohol hit her and everything felt so right, Coyia was breathing on Ant's neck and that made him horny. He thought she was doing it on purpose, so he took a chance and kissed her neck softly. That felt so good to Coyia that she turned her neck more. That's all Ant needed to see and he took full advantage of the situation and kissed and licked and sucked on Coyia's neck until her nipples got hard. Coyia pushed his hand down toward her booty and Ant grabbed it tightly. Coyia didn't take her time grabbing his dick either.

His dick was long and hard and Coyia ain't seen ant in a while and that made her sweet spot juicy. Ant wanted to be in control, so he pulled her hands away from his dick and he bent down to suck on her breast. Coyia helped him by pulling her bra down and helped him position himself without her shirt or bra being in the way. After sucking on her nipples and tities for a while Ant stood up and told her to make her way to the couch. She did as she was asked and walked over to the couch. Ant started taking of his shirt and Coyia laid down on the couch and did the same thing. Ant dropped to his knees and started sucking on her juicy fat pussy, and boy was it sweet wet. Coyia was not expecting that from him and that turned her on to the max. She never met a guy who went down on a woman first, or should I say without being asked or begged to after sucking their dick. That was an A+ and Coyia's book, and that made her want Ant even more.

Ant knew exactly what he was doing and he was driving her crazy to the point of no returns. She squirmed from side to side trying to catch her breath. She grabbed the back of his head tightly as she felt her climax building up. Her eyes rolled to the back of her head and her body tensed up and she squirted all over his face. She crossed her legs around his neck, almost choking him to death. Ant stopped sucking and popped his head up and said "Damn you trying to kill me girl"?

Coyia laughed and said while being out of breath "I'm sorry, it's been a long time, since, I been with someone, damn, I'm sorry, my bad boo keep going ". Anthony asked "do you want me to stop" Coyia's head popped up and she said in a angrily mood "No, why would you stop, don't stop"! Ant just laughed and went back to handling business. Ant stop sucking and looked at

Coyia and asked her "I guess the alcohol had a lot to do with this, right? Coyia just laughed and cover her face, and he went back to sucking on her sweet spot. Coyia was on cloud nine, her body felt good and Ant head game was the bomb. She was floating in her own puddle of juices and loved every moment of it. She came at least 5 times and he was still going. Ant finally stopped and pulled away and said "I have to use the bathroom". He got up, blew out the candles on his way down the hall and made it completely dark in the living room and guided himself down the hall by touching the walls on the way to the bathroom. When he got to the bathroom he shut the door and it sounded like a phone rang, but Coyia was too tired to get up and look for her phone. Her body was shaking from so many orgasms she just laid there and fantasized about her life to be with her new man. She even plans on making life easy for him in so many ways.

Coyia wasn't going to suck his dick at least not tonight, but shit he earned it and she already made it up and her head to please her soon to be man and every way he wanted needed and desired. She was ready to do what it took to please and to keep Ant. She told herself she wasn't going to hold back once he got back in the room, she was going to take control and suck his dick. she closed her eyes and thought about all her tricks she learned over the years, just then she heard the toilet flush and a door open and close. She said with a soft voice" come here I want to suck your dick now" and his dick hit her in the face. She turned her body and grabbed ahold of his dick and swallowed it whole. She licked it, spit on it, kissed it, she even tickled his balls with her fingers and licked them with her tongue from side to side. She told herself that she was going all in, and that's exactly what she did.

Coyia made sure she punished his dick with her mouth. she pushed his dick way back to the back of her throat and moaned. she would take it out every so often to catch her breath, then would go back to work. After a while sucking and tickling his dick, Coyia heard a door open and shut. Coyia stopped sucking his dick and looked through the dark hall and started sucking his dick louder to let ant brother know that they were busy. She paid no attention to his brother because she knew his brother couldn't see anything if he came into the front room.

She did start moaning loudly to give him a warning that they were busy. Coyia figured he was about to nut because he kept trying to pull away from her. So he told her to bend over and let him hit it from the back. Coyia did as she was told. Ant stuck his dick in and Coyia said "Oh Shit."

Coyia said while gripping the couch with her nails. Ant fucked the shit out of her, he would pull out every so often and would go back to beating Coyia's pussy up. Coyia was shaking because of the things he was doing to her. First, he would beating up and boy did it turn her on, then he would stop and go gentle and soft in loving. At first it felt like he came inside of her, so she reached back and he pulled out and she said, "Come here" and she turned around and grabbed his dick and to her surprise he had on a condom so she didn't stress it because he was beating it up just how she liked it. She heard a noise in the hallway and said, "I think your brother is coming in and out of the room?" Ant replied, "Don't sweat it".

As he came and she came as well. They cuddled up together and passed out on the couch. Coyia woke up like an hour later and put on her clothes to go to the bathroom and to check on

Ant's brother Rell. She wanted to make sure he wasn't going through her stuff. She opened her bedroom door and cut on the lights only to see Rell laying sideways on her bed, asshole naked.

She was furious, but didn't want to wake Ant so she walked around the room to make sure he didn't go through any of her things. She was about to raise hell when Rell got up but didn't want to lose Ant at the same time. So she said to herself "If this Nigga don't flash they both gone when they get up". She was on the way out of the room and noticed his dick was white like he came or something. She couldn't help it, she flashed. "Nigga, get yo dirty ass up out my house"!

Rell jumped up and said, "Huh what, what, what happen'? Coyia said, "Nigga get your punk ass out my motha fuckin house now"! "Nigga how dare you lay in my bed naked"? "Nigga we ain't fuckin"! "Who the fuck do you think you is"? "Get your shit and get the fuck out my house now"! "Ant come in here now"! Rell didn't mean to fall asleep, but Coyia had some good pussy and he laid down to think about it and passed out. Rell said, "I'm sorry, please calm down". But Coyia wasn't having that. She yelled "Ant, get in here now and get your pervert ass brother out of my house now"! Ant walked into the room and saw his brother putting on his clothes and said,

"What's going on in here bro"? Coyia said, "Do you even have to ask"?

"Look at your brother in my motha fuckin bed naked". Ant said "what's good, why are you naked"? With a smirk on his face. Rell kinda smiled and Coyia saw both of their faces and that pissed her off. She looked at Ant and saw him smiling and said, "Both of y'all get out my house". By then Rell was dressed and walked by her and said, "We got ours so hey, bye." Coyia was puzzled and replied" "what Nigga"? They both walked out of the room and into the living room and out the front door laughing and shaking hands. Coyia just slammed the door behind them and went to her room to pull all the covers and sheets off her bed.

When she pulled the covers and sheets off the bed, Rell's phone fell on the floor and on the front screen was a message from Ant that said, "Bro the lights are off go in there and hit it while she still feeling good and don't say a word just tap me lightly, but wait until I flush the toilet to go out. Coyia's heart dropped out of her chest. She felt dirty, used and taken advantage of. She was raped and didn't even know it. Coyia hurt deep down in her soul and all she could do was cry. She asked herself "why did this have to happen to me out of all people "? I go to church, I don't do people bad", she cried and cried and asked, "why me God"? The more she cried about it the more she thought about it. She knew this would eventually get out and she did not want her name in the streets as being a nasty ho. While Coyia cried and clinched Rell's phone she thought maybe she could find something in his phone to stop these punk bitch ass niggas from running their mouths. She scrolled down and read all of rell's text messages. After going through Rell's phone she realized they had done this to other girls and this made her angry. She called most of the girls and told them exactly what had happened to her and explained that it had happened to them and wanted to make a plan to fuck them up somehow, someway! One of the girls she told went crazy, she screamed, "I knew that wasn't just him"! She cried and thanked Coyia and they both cried together and felt for each other as if they were sitting in the same room with each other. Coyia hung up the phone, went to the closet in the hallway and grabbed some sheets and covers. She made up her bed and put new pillow cases on the pillows and got in bed. She put a pillow between her legs and one in front of her and held onto the pillow tightly as if she was holding someone. She cried herself to sleep and passed out.

So Coyia woke up the next morning and cleaned her house and vowed to herself that she was done with men. After she got done cleaning, Coyia got dressed and just didn't want to be bothered with anyone or anything. She turned her phone and silent, locked her doors, got into her car and drove into the spa. She wanted to make sure she didn't miss anything from those dirty dogs. She planned on taking this to the grave and she hoped they would do the same if they knew better. She laughed to herself and said, "Only if they knew what was coming to them, once Dot finds out about it, and for doing that to his only little sister, I hope they die, I want them to pay for what they did to me and so many other girls". After finishing up with the spa she decided to go buy a new outfit. She was trying her hardest to take her mind off of yesterday. She was on her vacation from work and didn't want to waste it on some childish ass niggas that play kid games.

Coyia walked through the mall and glanced at some dresses and a few stores. Coyia had on a black sweat suit with a matching top and her all black jordan. She found a store that had a going out of business sign and walked in there to look around. As soon as she walked in the store she saw some stilettos that she liked and decided to change her whole outfit in the mall. She picked out a pair of white jeans with black stilettos and a black shirt that said, (I'm all I need) on it.

She looked in the mirror and smiled when she saw herself and said, "Damn I'm a queen bee and the bees are always chasing this honey today". She walked out of the store she was in and went to the food court to find something to eat. She decided on getting a Subway sandwich to save some money and while in line she heard someone say something to her in a sweet and sexy tone and said, "Damn if you ain't the sexiest woman I have ever seen and you working the fuck out of that outfit beautiful!" Coyia smiled and said "shit, I better be, this shit cost an arm in a leg, but was supposed to be on clearance". They both laughed and the guy reached out his hand to her and said "My name is Rob and you are"? Coyia looked at his hand and said "i'm not interested but thanks and nice to meet you rob". Rob said "come on lil mama, I ain't trying to be your man just yet, but I would like to meet a new friends and the way you looking right now in that skirt, I wouldn't mind just walking along side you being your male best friend". Coyia thought about it for a second and wanted her space, but she thought why not walk with someone in the mall so no one else got at me. Coyia took out her hand and said "find, but my answer ain't changing my name is coyia".

Rob smiled and said "no problem". "Will Ms Coyia, can I buy your food for you? Coyia said "No I don't need anyone to buy my food, I'm a big girl and a grown women". I can and don't mind doing it for myself, but thanks for the offer, what's your name again Todd right"?

Coyia smiled and paid for her food and walked off. Rob jumped out of line and ran after Coyia. "My name is Rob and can you slow down for a minute so we can converse and I can get you to your car safely please"? Coyia looked back at him and continued to walk to the exit. Rob caught up to coyia and out of the bloe coyia said "I want you to know I don't have time for a man, niggas, boyfriend, best friends or whatever ya'll are are dogs, man, ya'll scandalous and I don't have time for no one that's not ready to settle down and be real and that can treat me like a queen that i am". Rob saw that she had been hurt by someone recently. She either got left or cheated on or just plain old man problems, but he knew actually what to do to fix that problem or at least get her to see him. Coyia walked out the exit door and started crying silently with tears rolling down her face. Rob saw her crying and just grabbed Coyia hand and swung her around to him and hugged her tightly. Coyia tried to push him away, but Rob's hold was too tight. Coyia yelled "get the fuck off me, move man

I'm okay". Rob started talking in a calm voice saying "it's okay, let it out", whatever happened to you just let it out", while he was still hugging her. Coyia just gave in and stopped fighting and broke down. To be honest it felt good and Coyia couldn't fight the tears back anymore, she just cried and hugged him back. Rob said in a low but soothing voice "lil mama I don't know what happened to you or what you've been through but I got you, let it out".

After a few minutes of crying, Coyia's nose was runny and her makeup was all over Rob's shirt. Coyia pulled her head away a big snot booger pop. Rob saw the bubble and said in a funny voice "awe damn man," in a very funny voice. Coyia busted out laughing and pushed Rob away and wiped her nose with her shelve and said "I hate you already for making me cry and I don't even know ". Rob smiled and said "My bad, I just saw it all over your face, she laughed again and said "thank you for that, i really need that but i gotta go". Rob grabbed her hand and asked for her phone number just in case she wanted to talk to someone and to get some shit off her chest.

Coyia wasn't trying to be around any more men. She just had two bad nights and needed to get her mind right. Rob said "how about I put my number in your phone and you call me when you want to, anytime you want to talk, i'm here and you'll always have this shoulder to cry on because that bubble claimed it already They both laughed and Coyia handed Rob her phone and he put his phone number and her phone and called himself. Coyia said "oooo, you were slick for that, how do you know I wanted you to have my number"? Rob said" I didn't, just want to keep in contact with you that's all." Coyia turned around and said "That's my car right there, but I'll call you when I have time okay" Rob grabbed her hand and kissed it and said "I'll be waiting on it to have a nice day, ms Coyia it was a pleasure meet you today". Coyia smiled, opened her car door and got in her car. Rob closed her door and walked out the way for Coyia to drive off.

Rob knew he had her already, he said to himself "I need her on my team, shit the more the merrier," and walked back into the mall to order him some food. On his way to get his food he started thinking to himself," shit she's already broken and wide open, shit I got that one." "All I have to do is put her back together". Rob turned around and said "Fuck this food shit i have to go pick this money up from this bitch real quick. He turned around to head back to the parking lot. Rob was what you could call a player. To others he was a pimp because people always seen him with so many different women and he got money out of all of them. He didn't call himself that because to him all pimps did was flash their nice cars, wore loud clothes and beat bitches, or at least the ones he saw. Rob was taught by his cousin smooth that was a real pimp, but he was a smooth ass dude that didn't beat females or ever raise his voice, all he had to do was look at them a certain way and they knew what time it was once that happened. Rob stayed around family, his bitches and around pimps to stay on point. We all know the saying birds of a feather flock together is what I was told, but he told himself he wasn't a pimp. Rob was a laid back kind of guy that loved his family, loved having a good time drinking, playing cards or dominos with close partner's. He loved being alone because he was a thinker and thought of all kinds of ways to make money from street shit or legitimate business shit. He loved talking about old memories and how his family was together and strong, but most of all he loved making money and stacking his bread. Rob was 5'9 with a dark chocolate complexion. He weighs about 180 soaking wet and had a body that was naturally ripped and cut. He had wave that went all the way around his head and always match from head to toe. Rob felt like he could have any women he wanted. He loved when they played hard to get because that meant he had to really use his game and he loved a challenge. He loved the cat and mouse chase because in the end he always got what he wanted and that turned him on better than getting money. Always knowing he never ran out of games and would never be broke because he always had something to say to someone and that meant he would never be broke.

Coyia got home and went straight to her room with her food. She sat her food on the dresser so that she could take off her new stuff she just bought. She said to herself, "I'll be damned if I spill something on this skirt, but I will be wearing this the next time I go out." Then she picked up the remote controller from the TV stand up and grabbed her food and sat down on the bed to watch TV while she ate her food. She flipped through the channels for something to watch, but couldn't find anything good. Just when she was about to pick something to watch her phone rang. Coyia grabbed her phone and smacked her lips and answer the phone screaming "Your punk bitch ass nigga don't you ever call my phone again, how dare you call my phone after what you in your bitch ass brother of yours did to me, I hate you and hope you die a slow painful death bitch, and if I was you, I would be watching my back from here on out cause you might get shot bitch and don't every call my phone again"! and hung up and blocked his number and turned her cell phone off for the night and at that very moment she sat back with her knees to her chest feeling anger and rage which brought tears to her eyes. At that moment all she could do was cry and think how they mistreated her and violated her. They destroyed something inside of coyia that day. Coyia laid down and looked at the TV hoping that would take her mind off of those two clowns and some movie was on that seemed old but it helped seeing a man get his leg beat together with a sledgehammer. Coyia watched as much as she could until she passed out.

Coyia woke up at 10 o'clock in the afternoon and looked at the TV screen only to see a different movie on. "She said, damn, next time I'll record that fucking movie." Weeks went by with Coyia just sleeping and not answering her phone. She got to the point where she was dirting her house on purpose just to have something to do. She quit her job and would only talk to Nikki so she wouldn't come over. She always told nikki she had something to do the next day so nikki wouldn't pop up and drag her out the bed. Coyia woke up at 10 o'clock in the afternoon and looked at the TV screen only to see a different movie on. "She said, damn, next time I'll record that fucking movie." Coyia grabbed her phone and looked through it. She noticed she had 4 missed calls, one of them were private and the other two were from her cousin Nikki and she had a call from Las Vegas that she didn't recognize at all. She thought out loud and said "I wonder who this is, and I hope it ain't no bill collector, or I'm hanging up," and she called the Las Vegas number back. while Coyia waited for someone to pick up the phone she sat up and yawned. A guy answered the phone and said "I'm glad you called me back sweet lady, how is your morning going?" Coyia couldn't recognize his voice at all, She said "who is this," and the guy replied, "So now you don't remember my voice huh?" Coyia said "look it's too early to be playing and not to be rude but I just woke up and I cant recognize your voice, so if I was you I would say my name before I hang up on you." He said "Damn like that mama, after we had a kodak moment in the mall, this is what I get for lending you my shoulder". A smile came across her face and Coyia said "Ooooooooo I don't remember your name". "O yea", I remember now, "they both started laughing". Coyia asked him "Ain't your name like booger or something like that"? He replied It's rob, not Robby, not robert, or booger". Good try though." Coyia said "My bad," Rob said no disrespect intended though. Rob asked "what are you getting into today," Coyia said "I don't know, I ain't got nothing planned for today." Rob said "send me your address and ima come pick you up so we can go get something to eat and converse." Coyia said "Who said I was hungry and why do you think I want you to know where I live, you could be a stalker and a killer for all I know." Rob just laughed and said "okay, how about you meet me at McDonalds and we'll go from there," Coyia thought about it and said," why McDonalds out of all places to go," Rob said" because it in a public place in you don't trust people right now". So instead of trying to debate on a spot to go we'll start there so I can earn your trust and we can get to know each other". Coyia ``okay, but don't expect me to get all dressed up cause this is short notice," Rob laughed again and said," man just threw some clothes on and come on i'll meet you at the McDonalds," Coyia said "which McDonalds"? he said "the one by the Lloyd center", Coyia said "okay, I'll be there in 15 to 20 minutes," and Rob said "okay" they hung up. Coyia jumped out of bed and ran into the bathroom to turn on the shower. She started brushing her teeth and pulling her clothes out at the same time.

Coyia got out of the shower and lotion up real fast and threw on her clothes. she had on black sweats with some all black forces and a black tee shirt that said on it "DON'T HATE!" She put her hair in a ponytail real quick and ran for the door. When she got to the front door she realized that she didn't have her phone or keys to lock up her house. She turned around and saw a light come on through the curtains in her back and thought about Ant and his brother, then she stopped right in her tracks, but then thought it could have been a cat or some type of animal, so she shook it off and ran to her room and got her phone and keys. Before she left her house she looked through the curtains in her kitchen just to make sure nobody was there. She looked out the window and didn't see anything so she ran out the door and locked up her house and drove to McDonalds to meet a new friend. She got in her car and started the car so that it was warmed up, but before she drove off, she checked her phone. She said "Fuck, I'm late but Shit I don't care I ain't trying to meet nobody right now anyways, so if he's gone then hey, I ain't lost nothing but a possible headache". When she pulled up she saw Rob sitting at the table eating and was kind of surprised he was still there waiting for her. Coyia found a parking spot and walked inside of the McDonalds in a hurry cause she knew she was late, but didn't want him to think she had him waiting so long on purpose.

She walked up to him and said "I'm so sorry, but I had to take a quick shower, that's just not me to just step out the house dirty smelling bad". Rob smiled and said "I ain't sweating it, I figured out what you were doing cause I would've done the same thing, but don't let it happen again". They both laughed but little did she know Rob was serious about what he said and Rob asked her what she wanted to eat on the menu. Coyia smiled and said "I thought we were just meeting here, and going to find somewhere to eat together," Rob took a bite of his burger and smiled. He chewed his food and stared at Coyia. Coyia said "why are you looking at me like that," Rob got done chewing and said "You don't see me eating, and you messed that up already by being late, so go order anything you want from the dollar menu." and he smiled. Coyia smiled and said "Are you serious?" Rob shook his head and said" yea I ain't playing, I planned on taking you out, then 10 minutes passed and then you never showed up. So after 20 minutes passed and I decided to order, I figured you flaked on me, so I ordered and said maybe next time." Coyia smiled then got up and ordered a drink of ice tea and came back to the table and said "I ain't hungry, but thanks anyways, but what you can do is, tell me a little bit about yourself"? Rob asked with his mouth full of fries ``why don't you tell me about yourself since I'm eating, if you don't mind". Coyia said "What do you want to know"? Rob said "Everything there is to know about you, Coyia, like where are you from, what's your favorite color, what kind of music you listen to, what is your favorite food, movies, pets, you know stuff like that"?

Coyia stared at Rob for a while with a smile on her face, she pondered on all the questions he had just asked her and said "why do you want to know all that now, here, at McDonalds, that's not kind of funny". "I mean this ain't even a real date"? Rob stared at her with a straight and direct stare, then said "Why does that seem strange to you, I mean we're at a restaurant, eating, well I'm eating you chose not to and we're only here because you were late so I decided to grab a bite to eat." "So to answer your question no it doesn't seem strange at all, this is the only way I know how to get to know someone and it's been working for me this long, so why should McDonalds, or any place or thing stand in my way of getting to know a beautiful woman like yourself". "I mean you did almost stand me up as late as you were, so I feel like that's the least you can do to make it up to me, don't you think"? Coyia smiled because he was right, but she was thinking to herself ``I don't owe you a thing, but being that I was late,

I could give him a little insight on myself". "Okay you know my name already and I don't have any ", just as she was about to finish what she was saying Rob's phone rang and stopped Coyia right in her mid-sentence. He said give me a second, my bad and Coyia shook her head as Rob answered the phone. Coyia expected him to walk off like every guy does, but he sat there and talked. So Coyia turned her head so she could hear if it was a male or female he was talking to, but she didn't want to seem like she was noisy. When Coyia looked at Rob, his face turned from happy to mad and his forehead crinkled up like he didn't like what he was hearing. Rob said to his phone "Bitch, I can give three fucks about you or those bitches, just cause one of yall went to jail doesn't stop nothing, yall better get it together and get my money or we gon have problems, now try me if you want too, faggot ass bitch, and he hung up". When Coyia heard that her head whipped in his direction and looked away again.

Before he hung up he had a frown on his face that said he was really pissed but as soon as he hung up the phone he acted as if nothing was wrong. Coyia looked at Rob and asked, "Is everything alright," Rob smiled and said "Great, now where were we"? Coyia just stared at rob, cause she wanted to ask him who he was talking to, but didn't want to be noisy, but right as she was about to start talking he answered her question. "I bet you're wondering who I was talking to like that"? Coyia wanted to say yeah, but didn't want him to think she was too noisy, Coyia smiled and said "Kind of, but I ain't trying to be in your business like that". Rob said "I manage a lot of women on the streets and that's how I get my change". Coyia said "so you're a pimp"?

Rob said nah, not a pimp, I'm an entrepreneur, but in so many words, a lot of people would call it that". Coyia looked at him in disbelief. She asked, "How did you know I wanted to know who you were talking too"? Rob started laughing, and said "for one what women on this earth wouldn't want to be the only one, for one, for two I was staring at you while I was talking, yo head swung in disbelief". Coyia said "why are you telling me this"? Rob responded, because I want you to know I have nothing to hid, either you're going to except me for who i am or not, that your issue and choice, but I would like to get to know you a lot more better without running game on you or lying to you, giving you that choice to know the truth about me before we go any further". Rob said "I know you're not a hoe that's why I'm trying to get to know you instead of flashing my money in your face or running some good game on you". Coyia smiled and said, "that's good to know cause I ain't no hoe, but I do give you props because a lot of men would try to run a game too, but I would have left before they got two words out their mouth". Rob cut her off and said, "lil mama, I know you ain't no hoe, we both know this, I just want someone to chill with and be normal with, you know someone I can tell my problems to and not worry about them telling my business to the rest of the world, i true girl friend, You know someone who will cherish my words and not judge me because of what I have or do, you think you can be that person or am i just wasting my time"? Coyia's heart kind of felt good knowing that his intentions wasnt to pimp on her, and now it was her turn to receive help from someone instead of always helping others for a change.

She looked deep into Rob's eyes and could sense something coming from his eyes. She didn't know what it was, sincerity or envy or maybe just sympathy but it hit a spot and she fell for it. As she stared at Rob and he put his head down and Coyia thought to herself,(I guess I can give him a shot, I ain't got nothing to lose, and he might even school me on something about men, or give me the game, I'll give him a shot at this friend thing). Coyia said "okay, fuck it why not, but you remember this, I ain't no hoe and will never hoe for any man on this earth, I don't need a man to pay my bills or help me manage my hard earned money, I have dreams and goals in life and I plan to get shit done and accomplish them". Rob had a smile on his face and said "Okay sexy lady I understand, but will pick this up on another day I gotta go check this trap from these bithces before they run off with it, I'll see you when you're ready to link up again or just call me, okay". Coyia said okay and they got up. She said "Why don't you just ask me what I'm doing tomorrow"? Rob said "Okay what you doing tomorrow then"? Coyia smiled and said "Meeting you with you", Rob gave her a hug and said "okay bet, but this time don't be late or I'll leave you". They both laughed and walked each other out to their cars and went their separate ways. While Rob was walking to his car he had a devilish grin on his face, knowing it was just a matter of time before he would have her and eventually turn her out to the game as well. Coyia walked to her car with a smirk as well, she knew he'll try to pimp on her eventually, but she was about to watch him and ask as many questions as she could before that time came, then she planned on splitting and getting as far away from him as she could. As Coyia got in her car she kept saying to herself ``Don't get too attached" she knew he had a sweetheart but she wanted to make sure she never got played again and he was going to give her what she needed to know about the game and men. When Coyia got home she walked inside her house, locked her door and went straight to her book collection to see what she had on pimping. She didn't find many books but she did watch a lot of movies on pimping so she went to her movie collection to see what she had. She found a couple of movies and she took them to her room and sat them on her DVD player and said "Tomorrow I'll start pimpoly," she took her clothes off and got in bed and went to sleep.

Rob got to the motel where two of his females were and called one of them to bring him his [trap] aka [money], he told her he was in the parking lot and to hurry up. The girl came out of the room running with just a bra on and some booty shorts that made her ass stick out. She was a white pretty girl with a slim fit body she had hips and ass to die for. She stood about 5'5 and weighed no less than 140 soaking wet, the girl was every man's dream but drugs and homelessness got the best of her and Rob gave her everything she needed to keep going. She ran up to his car and knocked on the window. He stepped out of the car and grabbed the money from her. He counted the money fast in his head and looked up at her and said "Where is the rest of my money bitch," as he grabbed her by the hair and pulled her toward him. The girl yelled "agh, daddy that's all we made so far, but we both got two licks on the way so everything will be right I promise, daddy please". Rob whispered violently in her ear, "you raggedy bitches better have my money in one hour, or it's going to be a problem, do I make myself clear," she said "Yes daddy", and he let her go, she started walking fast back into the motel room. Rob got in his car and drove off and went to the closest bar to have a drink.

Morning couldn't have come sooner for Shacoyia. She was up before the birds and she was preparing herself for the day. She had found two pimp books called [pimpoly] by pimpin ken and a book called [pimp] by Iceberg slim and four pimp movies called the Mack, American pimp 1 and 2 and a documentary by Iceberg slim called black widow. Coyia didn't know where to start or what to look for so she just popped in a movie and grabbed a book and started reading and watching the movie at the same time. She thought she would eventually find something that made sense to her. Eventually, she watched two out of four movies and scammed through both books and got bits in pieces from both books and movies. She didn't understand why these girls just didn't make the money and leave cause they all could have done it for themselves and kept the money, Coyia was confused. She couldn't understand how these women could accept being dogged and mistreated by a man, and yet still go back to him and still pay his pockets, Coyia shocks her head in disbelief. She said out loud to herself, "This shit, is unbelievable", and she was right. By the time she scammed through the books and watched most of the movies, she was tired and drained. Coyia had fallen asleep and didn't mean to. When Coyia had woken up, it was two o'clock in the afternoon, and she said to herself, "I might as well get dressed, so I can call this man". Coyia learned from those movies and books that those females are misled, misguided and lost, and she swore to herself that that would never be her. She knew a lot of those girls fell for the okie doke because of the flashy diamonds and jewels, and cars and money, but she thought why wouldn't they want the same for themselves instead of having the man looking all good. Coyia didn't understand and didn't want to understand, she just knew it wasn't going to be her period. After Coyia got dressed, she called Rob to see if they were still kicking it today. She called his number. The phone rang about three times and Rob answered the phone, "Who this",

Coyia looked at the phone expecting him to know who it was with a puzzled look on her face, she said "Is that how you answer the phone these days", Rob smiled because he knew none of his bitch would ever talk to him like that, cause if they did they would have gotten there ass beat or cussed out real quick like. He smiled through the phone and said "Naw, what's going on sexy, how is your day going, and what's on your agenda for today"? Coyia smiled and said "You tell me, you're the one with all the big moves and hoes, pimp." They both laughed and giggled, but Rob laughed cause he believed in the law of attraction and what she just did was call him pimp. Soon he knew that she would be his and that he would eventually break her for everything she has plus more, it was just a matter of time.

He asked "Where do you live, I'm about to come get you now"? Coyia thought about it for a second and said to herself "Why am I worried, I won't be selling my body for nobody", and she gave him her address "okay I live on 27th and killingsworth across the street from that church in the blue townhouse". Rob said "I'll be there in ten minutes be ready and he hung up".

Coyia looked at the phone and said "ooookkkk ayyyy", and hung the phone up. While she waited for Rob to come get her, she made sure all her windows in doors were shut in locked. She grabbed her coat and purse and headed out the door to stand on the front porch. She locked the front door and sat on the porch and not too much longer Rob pulled up with his music blasting.

Coyia walked to the car as fast as she could and said "Damn, turn that down I do have neighbors". Rob laughed and said "my bad baby, that's just how I drive"! Coyia said "Will please respect me and please don't come here like that again, I have to live here and don't need no complaints for these nosey neighbors". Rob reached down and turned the music all the way down and started driving off, he seem she had some kind of attitude, and he tried to make her smile by reaching for her face and saying "Are you mad sugar bear my bad baby". Coyia moved her face away from his hand and swung her hand to move his hand from her face. She laughed and said "move boy, before I hurt you," and they both laughed. Rob drove down a couple of block before blasting the music again, but instead this time he turned the music on full blast, so the world could hear it. They drove to a couple places, and got some food to go, but they talked a lot more and got to know each other a lot better. Rob had to swing by his homeboys house to pick up some money, but he didn't want Coyia thinking something weird was going on. So Rob asked Coyia if she wouldn't mind if he went to go pick up his money from his homeboy and from his bitches? Coyia shrugged her shoulders and said "I don't care," and they were off. Rob decided to go get his money from his bitches first because he didn't trust them. He pulled up to the motel and parked his car, picked his phone up and called for one of his females to bring out his money. He asked in one of the rudest ways if you asked me." Bring my money to me bitch". I could never be a hoe, especially if a man is talking to me like that, hell naw, honey. Coyia just stared at Rob, and he felt her stare but kept looking straight ahead. The most beautiful woman Coyia ever saw came out. She was counting the money so fast and speed walking to Rob's car.

When she got to the car she knocked on the window and waited until he rolled his window down. The girl handed Rob a stack of 20's and a stack of 50's and a stack of 100's and she stood there while he counted the money that was given to him. The girl bent over and looked at Coyia and said daddy, we got this bachelor party to go to in a couple hours and candy still in the room with her lick, what do you want me to do cause these bitches don't look right and they act like they don't want no money. Rob

Coyia jumped out his car and jumped into his truck real fast. Rob had a navigator sitting on 28's, it was candy apple red with tinted windows. When Coyia got into the truck it looked like he had to at least of spent fifty thousand easily on the inside of the truck it had t.v and beats and the softest seats you could ever sit on.

Coyia was adjusting the seat when Rob ran over to her and said hold on, he jumps in the passenger seat and grabbed a cd out the glove compartment. It had big letters on it that said G.P.M on the front cover of the C.D. He went through the songs until he got to this song called (whatever you want) and he jumped out the car in said tell me what you think about this song then he shut the door and got into his car and drove off. Coyia started rolling down the windows and the music started blasting in she jumped in her seat. Coyia turn the music down as fast as she could and grabbed her phone and said "He got me fucked up"! she called Rob and he said real quick "I'm stopped at the corner waiting for you", Coyia said "you and your music got me fucked up, you knew this fucking music was turned up like this when you got out the car, rob"!

Rob started laughing and said "O shit, my bad I be forgetting about my music, my bad," Coyia said "your damn right it's your bad, that shit scared the fuck out of me and almost blew out my ear drums, but I'm coming now where are you parked at right now". He said "I'm at the corner right here by the 711". Coyia said "Okay" and hung up the phone and backed out and drove off to where he was waiting for her at. While they drove from place to place Coyia listen to that cd and random songs came on, but Coyia only liked four of the songs one was called (**Exactly**), (**Getting my money**), (**So many ways**) and (**whatever you want**). Every so often Rob would look through his mirror only to see Coyia dancing to the music and he would smile cause he knew she was feeling that pimp shit. From the moment that Coyia started driving his car every head turned and everyone looked at Coyia driving his car, and she loved every bit of it. Coyia felt on top of the world, feeling all the vibration going through her body and as she listens to her new favorite song on that cd So many ways. Rob pulled up to a house on Mallory and Going and ran into a yellow house. He stayed in there no longer than a minute and he came out with a bag and jumped back into his car and continued to drive. Rob drove down a couple more blocks and pulled to the side and threw his arm out the window and signaled for Coyia to pull on the side of him. She did what he was signaling her to do with his arms and rolled down the window all the way. Rob said "When we pull up to this next house, jump back in this car and wait for me", Coyia said "Okay", and they drove off once again.

They drove down going past a school that had a lot of people just kicking it at and kids were everywhere. About six more blocks later he pulled over and Coyia did the same. She rolled all his windows up and locked all his doors and got into robs car. She handed him his car keys and he got out of the car and said that he would be right back. He ran into a light blue house and came outside with a light skinned girl. She must have been telling him something he liked to hear, because he had a big grin on his face and they kept on giving each other daps. The light skinned girl was loud and she kept on yelling "On everything cuddy", Rob cut her off and told her to go get her shoes and stuff so they could leave. Rob said to the light skinned girl in a low voice "I just bumped me a new one and I'm setting my traps so I need you to be real friendly.

The light skinned girl walked up to the car and said "Hey how are you doing"? Coyia said" fine and yourself"? the light skinned girl said "my name in Tee Tee what's your name"? "My name is Coyia" Tee Tee said. ``It was nice meeting you and trust me girl he's a good man, you should stick around," Coyia said "I'll try" they shook hands and Tee Tee walked to the car she was about to drive. Then she noticed that she didn't get her shoes and still had her house shoes on, and she forgot her coat. She honked the horn and ran over to Rob before he pulled off and said "Cuddy i'll just meet you there I forgot that I still had on my slipper and I didn't grab my coat yet", Rob said "Okay hurry up please and meet us at the motel please", she said" okay ", and ran in the house as they pulled off. Rob got around the corner and stopped the car he said "Grab me that DVD in there real quick, I make movies to, and I want you to watch it on the way back to the motel and give me your honest opinion on it, "okay" Coyia shook her head and a yes motion.

Rob made a movie on hoeing and the glamorous lifestyle that it came with. The movies started off with all his women at a motel with some of the players from the L.A Laker. They were turning up and having a great time, while making money. The movie shoulded them in different parts of the world and different states. They were always with some type of celebrity or famous person and Coyia was intrigued. As she watched on, Coyia saw women walking around with thousands of dollars in their hands and she was shocked. Some had clothes to die for and others had on hoe shit. That made Coyia really get into that movie. Every so often Rob would look over at Coyia just to see her facial expression, and he liked what he saw, but every so often he would ask her question like, "Could you see yourself going there? Or "You like that money you see, what could you use that for?" everything was taking Coyia by surprise because she thought hoeing was women getting beat and dogged by their pimps, but what she saw wasn't nothing like that. Coyia wouldn't answer but all she would do is shake her head when he talked to her, but would keep her head in the movie he made just for women like her. They pulled up to the motel and Coyia was still stuck in the movie, but Rob call all his bitches and told them to make their way outside in five minutes and hung up the phone. Rob asked Coyia if she liked the movie and she said "it was cool", then he asked her if she wanted to go make some money and at first she was shocked, but thought and said what do I have to do, Rob said nothing at all just go up there and see if you like it that's all. Coyia thought about it for a minute and asked "are you sure, because I'm against hoeing and you know this", and Rob put his hand and the air and said "Swear all you have to do is be you that's all".

Coyia said "alright then I'll go, just to see how shit works, but I swear I'm not doing anything". Rob smiled and said "okay". Rob honked the horn and all his hoes came running out the motel room, and just as they came out his cousin pulled up in his other car. There was a couple of girls that ran out first and Rob got out the car in walked up to them before they got to the car. He must have said something to them about Coyia because their eyes kept looking at Coyia then back at rob. They shook their heads and walked to rob's car and got inside. Rob walked up stairs and it seem like 10 girls came out that one room fixing some part of the body.

Eye brows, wigs, ponytails ass and titties, ect. All Coyia could do was laugh and introduce herself to the girls that had just got in the car. One of the girls reached her hand out and said "what's your name", Coyia turned around and said "my name is Coyia, and your name is", while shaking the girl's hand. "My name is diamond, and this is chocolate", Coyia turn around and shook chocolates hand and asked them, "How long have been with rob. Diamond said "I been here from Cali, hmm, about ten years and chocolate's been here for about 3 years, right", as she looked at chocolate while she shook her head and a yes motion. Coyia looked surprises and said "Yall been hoeing that long for rob", diamond said "Yep, it's actually coo, cause we travel a lot and we try all kinds of new food and we meet a lot of super stars and ball players all the time".

Chocolate tap diamond and said "Come on girl before everybody else come out here", and diamond pulled out some powder and molly and asked "Coyia do you use", Coyia said "Naw only with my girls because I get out of control if you know what I mean". The girls looked at each other and said "Bitch we got you and were your bitches now, hit this mixed shit, you'll love it, and trust me bitch I won't let shit happen to you, I promise". Coyia thought about it for a while. Before she did anything she made sure to call or send her cousin Nikki the address just in case something happen, or if couldn't no one find her. Diamond mixed the drugs together so they would feel really good, as they talked and got high the fuck you think you sticking that in," the guy said "Whoever wants to get paid and asked the girl for her name.

She answered "my name is Truly", stands for Truly yours but, go sit on the couch so I can get her ready for that monster", they laughed and Truly grabbed Coyia's hand and said "come here real quick, you're going to need this if you're going to fuck that". Coyia said "no, I want to play with that, wait no, don't leave"! Truly pulled her around the corner with her. Truly said "Coyia, girl drink this and snort this because you alone ain't taking all that dick by yourself", Coyia said "what you mean, im taking all of it", Truly said "so we fuckin that right, i mean if you still want to be somewhat tight you'll share", unless you want it to yourself and trust me your pussy will never be the same, so what you trying to do". Coyia thought about it and said okay, "but, don't do too much because I want him to be my man". That didn't sit to well with Truly, so she pulled out some drugs and said do u fuck with this shit here, Coyia looked at it and said "yea, give me a bump and Truly did as she was asked. Coyia said "this is powder and molly right"? Truly looked at her and said "yea", with a smirk on her face and kept the bumps coming.

Coyia laid back feeling really good and Truly said "I'll go get him", and she walked off and got the guy. Coyia was on cloud nine, and her body felt better than that. She forced herself to get up and find her way to the living room. When she got there, stumbling with every step and with barely any vision to see. she flopped on the couch and closed her eyes. Not too much longer after she passed out, Truly walked up to Coyia and said out loud to everyone in the room. "Who wants to see me eat this bitch out while I use my friend"? She grabs the guy dick. Everyone raised their hands and screamed "yeah". Truly started to strip Coyia from her clothes violently and while she was doing that Coyia had woken up, but was still dazed and higher than ever. A tear rolled down Coyia's eye because she couldn't move and couldn't fight back, her body felt numb. Truly started eating Coyia's pussy and the man went crazy, they though money from one end of the room to the next. Coyia for some strange reason welcomed the pleasure. Like her body was moving on its own, and if was as if Coyia had no control. Truly ate her pussy so good that Coyia squirted everywhere and boy were they turned on from watching.

The guy with the snake dicked walked up to Truly and tried to put his dick inside Truly's pussy but she stopped eating Coyia's pussy and she said "Why you sweating me, put yo dick in that bitches' mouth", he looked at Coyia and it looked like she was enjoying it so he walk over to Coyia and did as he was told. Coyia sucked his like she was in a possessed porno, and the way Truly made her body feel was on some next level shit. The guy took his dick out of Coyias mouth and told Truly to move and rammed his 14 inch dick inside Coyia. It hurt at first, but the pleasure it brought was to die for. Eventually Coyia passed out and didn't wake back up this time. When Coyia finally woke up the room was trashed and no ones was in there with her. She tried to stand but couldn't, her body was so sore and bruised from the waist down. Coyia felt wet between her legs and pulled up her dress and put her hand between her legs and felt a lot of wetness and saw a lot of blood on her hand. She seen it coming from her pussy, but felt the pain in her ass. Blood poured out of her from both holes, her ass and her vagina and Coyia cried. She cried harder then she ever did. The pain that she was experiencing was unbearable and her body was weak. She tried to stand but could find the strength to move. Coyia looked around the room for her purse, she spotted it across the room and screamed out loud, fuuuccckkk! She knew she had to get to her purse because her phone was inside it. Coyia crawled with the little strength she had left in her, all the way across the room until she got to where her purse was. She pulled herself up to the bar and saw her face. Coyia couldn't believe what she looked like, and who in their right minds would ever do something like this to a person. She was shocked and hurt. Her soul cried and her tears came down her face faster then, when she saw all the blood coming out of her. Her whole upper body was covered in seaman. Coyia started shaking and begging god why. She grabbed her purse and opened it only to see robs text that read, (LOOK IMA NEED MY CUT SINCE YOU DECIDED TO STAY UP THERE WITH THOSE NIGGAS). Coyia couldn't believe her eyes, rage filled her and anger on top of all that shit she read robs signature on his phone read (IT'S A DIRT GAME). she never even noticed that, but for some reason she paid close attention to it now more than ever. She was exhausted, but knew if she didn't call someone she would probably die right there in that hotel suite living room all alone. She called the police and as soon as she started talking her phone died. Coyia was in pain, and cried out loudly all of sudden the lights went out and she fell to the floor dying in her own puddle of blood mixed in with different types of seaman.

When Coyia woke up, she looked around only to see she was in the hospital. She pulled the covers up hoping that everything she thought she remembered was a dream. She put her hands in between her legs and felt the stitches along the side of her vagina. Then she put her hands a little bit farther and felt the same thing around her ass. Tears fell from her face and she hated herself because this wasn't supposed to happen to her. She grabbed the pillow and screamed at it. While she was screaming the nurse walked in the room and said "O, you're up, sorry for disturbing you, but I have to check your wounds and change the badges". Coyia wiped her face and said "Sorry, I'm just hurt and I'm mad at the same time, but please tell me I don't have any S.T.D's please"? The nurse said she would check the chart after she was done changing her bandages. All Coyia could do was cry, she prayed at that very moment and bugged GOD for her not to have anything. The nurse got done and went to get her chart from outside at the nurse's station. When she return with her chart she stood in front of the bed and said "I don't see that you have any S.T.D's, but I do see that you had to get over 80 stitches from the inside of you and outside, all the way to your rectum", Coyia said I know I felt that all ready in low voice. The nurse continued and said "You also had a lot of drugs in your system, I see heroin, cocaine, molly, alcohol, crystal meth, ecstasy, now I see how

50

you called the police, and to be honest with you, your actually lucky to be alive cause your vitals was off the charts and your heart rate was near death, that's how slow it was going". "God really had to be on your side because, I never saw anyone that was this close to death and called the police for themselves. Coyia asked the nurse "Did they bring my purse here," the nurse said "Yes it's right over here in this hospital bag, the police wanted to take it but the nurse that was on before I got here said you might need some way to get home and the other officer said the purse and phone was on you at the time so they let you keep it". Coyia said "thank you guys I really appreciate it, Can you please hand it to me, I know my family is worried about me"? The nurse walked around the bed and handed the hospital bag to her and said to Coyia on her way out, "make sure you get a lot of rest because your body needs to heal and when I come back in, I'll give you some more morphine". Coyia said "okay" and grabbed her phone out of her purse inside the bag and saw a lot of hundred dollar bills in her purse all she said to herself was "was it worth it Coyia," and tears started falling from her eyes.

When she got herself together, she looked at her phone and saw ten messages all from Rob and like five missed calls from him. Coyia closed her eyes and cried herself to sleep. When Coyia got home she felt safe and scared at the same time. Safe because she was home in her own bed, but scared because Rob kept calling her and he knew where she lived and she didn't want this weird as dude coming to her house for a punk as 5500 dollars. By the grace of GOD, he never did. After months went by of being in the house healing Coyia got bored but was too scared to go out alone. The only time she would go out is to go to the grocery store or to her cousin Nikki's house. She loved her best friend but envied her because she had everything that Coyia wanted and when they were young she was just as nasty as she was back in the day.

Now don't get it wrong she loved her cousin and wanted the best for her, she just wanted everything she had. So nine times out of ten she would show up and pull Nikki out the house to go somewhere with her so she wasn't sitting in there house cupcaking in eachothers face. In reality she loves Nikki and everything she had, she knew her time was coming and wanted it and planned on having it one day. So Coyia stayed home and worked as much as she could on walking right. She cleaned her house until there was nothing more to clean then she started watching movies and that's when shit got real boring. It seems like every hour on the hour this movie kept coming on called (misery). She would only watch bits in pieces of the movie and would always pass out. The only reason why she would fall to sleep is because it was an older movie and it started out boring but she told herself that she would finish it one day. Days would go by and movies would get old after watching them over in over. So as Coyia flipped through the channels she saw that the movie misery was playing from the beginning and this time she decided to watch the whole movie this time. As she watched the movie, Coyia really got into it and when the movie was over, she screamed and said to herself "Damnnnn, I can see myself doing that to a man, if he pissed me off". She looked at her bed and said "shit, with the luck I got, I wouldn't mind locking a man to my bed right about now, shit I swear I would fuck the shit out of his ass", she laughed to herself all the way to the kitchen and made her self something to eat and got something to drink. She walked back to her room talking to herself saying "shit if that crazy as bitch can do it by herself, I know for damn sure I can too. she giggled to herself and kept talkimg to herself saying "shit, I wouldnt have done no stupid shit like that over no damn book tho, shit I would have fucked the dog shit out of his ass, shit thats why that bitch was so damn crazy because she was in no man land with all that damn snow, and no dick", Coyia laughed to herself and got back in bed with her snacks and restarted the movie from her DVR and call her cousin Nikki to tell her about the movie she just saw.

After weeks of staying home and watching as many movies she could watch. Coyia actually like being away from people and now she was starting to get restless. Coyia came walked in to her living room to water her flowers and her house phone rang. She answered the phone and said "hello," the voice on the other end said "how are you doing beautiful," Coyia asked "who is this" in a shocking voice, "It's Ant," Coyia's blood boiled and the veins in her forehead pop out. She screamed from the top of her lungs and said "Why the fuck is yo bitch ass call my phone, Bitch," Ant laughed and said "man, what is you tripping for, didn't nobody do nothing to you baby." Coyia balled her fist up and said "You son of a bitch, you going to sit here"! "No, didn't know body do nothing to you baby, what do you think we did to you"? "You punk bitch, you and that weak ass nigga took advantage of me, come on now, be a man about it and tell the truth, if you're a man, man up". "Hell naw, didn't nobody take advantage of you, everything we did was consensual and you know this". "Now, he did play with hisself in your bed and I know that was fucked up on his part and wrong, that part I know was scandalous on his behalf, but I didn't do anything to you". "I know I shouldn't have even brought him in the first place, I just figure that since yall ain't seen each other in a long time that you would be happy to see him, but didn't nobody do anything to you that you didn't want to happen to you, so don't make it seem like somebody raped you, cause didn't nothing happen like that, period"!

Coyia felt madness and anger coming from all parts of her body. She started crying and screamed "YOU STUPID MOTHERFUCKA, YOUR BITCH ASS BROTHER LEFT HIS PHONE IN MY BED AND I READ EVERYTHING YOU BITCHES DID TO ME, AND I HOPE YOU AND THAT BITCH AND ALL YOUR KID'S KIDS DIE AND YOU BURN IN HELL BITCH!" She slammed the phone down and cried to herself saying "Why did that nigga have to call me and fuck up my mood man damn, I hate him". Coyia sat there crying for a couple of minutes and jumped up and said "fuck it, I'm going to the first bar I see; I need a fucking drink like right now". She walked into her room and grabbed the first jumpsuit she had thought it on and grabbed her purse

E looked at her and said "I have no intention on trying to get with **you** or play games with you, I just seen you over her alone and right now it looks like you hate life because of what some weak as nigga did to you, but trust me I'm to that point in life, that I'm just looking for someone to talk too, that's all, can I do that if it's not too much to ask for." Coyia looked at and said "it's funny how you said the right things, with your EASY E looking ass". E smiled and said "that's what a lot of people call me". They both laughed and E handed the bartender a hundred-dollar bill and said "GEN keep em coming and just smiled because he was hard headed but it was in a cute way. As they talked and got to know each other a little, the alcohol started doing its job and Coyia loosened up alot. E was a funny guy and kept her laughing. While they were in a conversation someone came up to E and whispered something in his ear and he reached in his pocket and they guy handed him some money and E gave the guy something and the guy walked off happy. Now normally Coyia wouldn't have gotten into anyone's business but she was drunk and didn't really care. She asked him "What was that you said you did for a living?" E looked at Coyia and said "I never told you." Coyia smiled and said "your right, so what do you sell?" E said look in my lap," Coyia did as she was told and asked if that was crack in a low voice. E said "It coke, you fuck around with it"?

Coyia thought about what happen to her last time and said "I did, but something bad happen to me and now I don't fuck with nobody else's stuff". E said "will I do and if you decide to try some I'll be in the bathroom", and he got up and walked off toward the bathroom. Coyia thought about it and decide to follow him to the bathroom. She only did that because the alcohol kicked in and she was feeling it. She told him that she wanted to see it first and he handed everything to her. She smelled in and dipped her finger into it and tasted it. Her tongue got numb and she said "okay "you first", And he grabbed his key and did a big bump. He handed the key to Coyia and said "here you go". She did a small one and walked out the bathroom to make sure she wasn't getting drugged again.

E came out and asked her "So how was it," Coyia shook her head and said "It was cool." They sat there talking and enjoying each other company. E told Coyia he had to walk the room for a second but he would be right back. Coyia looked toward the door to see who he was looking at and saw a women come in their door waving at him to come outside. Coyia said "okay," and watched E walk the room shaking everyone's hand, like he was someone important and it kind of turned her on. He gave all kinds of women hugs with a small kiss on the check and gave all the man bro hugs. His smile brightens up the places and he was a magnet to the people. Coyia thought that's how her uncle pooh was when she was young she always said that she would have a man like that one day, but she wasn't rushing into this on like last time, and a part of her didn't even want to like him but it was something about him that kept her intrigued about him.

When E got back to the bar where Coyia was at, she said "So you're a superstar in here ain't ya." He smile and said "naw nothing like that, I just know I few people that's all", Coyia said "nigga who you think you trying to play, you just shook up the whole bar and some more, you must be one of those people that get around and that got 20 different baby mama's and a 1000 kids." E almost spit out his drink and said "Damn baby why so many, 20 baby mama's and a 1000 kids, naw ma, you got the wrong person baby". Coyia said "okay, but you ain't got to lie Craig, you ain't gotta lie." E said "I don't have any kids and no baby mama's it's just me in my family that's all baby". Coyia said "okay," but E had to leave, he had sold out and needed to go handle his business. So he wrote his number down on a napkin and said "Here's my number if you want to hang out." Coyia looked at his number and said "look, I'm done with man that mistreat women, pimp on women, or just want to treat us like toys, I'm not looking for a relationship, so don't be mad if I don't call you, but I do want you to know I had a good time tonight and you took all my problems away, but i'm not looking for anything right now, sorry E."

E said "okay I feel you, but this just came out your mouth, I helped you tonight and you came in here with the saddest face I ever seen in a long time, so ima write this down again and ima leave it right her on the counter and if you decide to take then that a win for both of us, if you decide not to take it then it was great spending time with you and getting to know you and i'm glad i helped you with your problems tonight, and thank you for letting me make you smile". E wrote his number on two napkins and handed one in front of Coyia and he balled the other one up and asked her to give him a hug before he left. When they stood up to give each other a hug he picked her up and spun her around while using his other hand to slide the napkin in her purse. He walked off saying have a great night with a sexy smile on his face and he walked out the bar with money still on the tab for coyia. Coyia finished her drink and looked at the number and said "If it's meant to be I'll see you again or get a sign from God or somewhere that it's time for me to get a man. Coyia stood up from her chair, looked at the number one last time and told the bartender to throw it away and she walked out the bar and got into her car and started heading home. While she drove to the freeway she got hungry and was looking for a fast-food place to eat. She thought about E while she drove, he seemed different and not like the others, she was kind of mad that she told the bartender to throw that boy's number away. She wanted to go back to get it, but didn't want to seem desperate. so she said "Fuck it, if I see him again then I'll take his number." She saw a small burger joint and decided to stop there to eat. She went through the drive thru and ordered a bacon burger with fries. Her order came up to 6 dollars and she reached for her purse only to see a balled up napkin. She opened it and saw E's number on it and she shook her head and laughed. It actually made her happy that he did that. She paid for her food and went home with a big smile on her face. Coyia got home and went into her room and finished her food while she watched T.V she flipped through the channels and saw the movie that she watched the other day called (MISERY). She finished her food and took off her clothes and passed out watching that movie.

Coyia fell into a deep sleep and dreamed about the movie she was just watching. It was a scary dream but different type of scary dream. She saw a man tied to her bed and he was screaming at her and calling her all kinds of bitches and hoes, but for some reason it was turning her on and she started playing with herself while he spits at her. She got horny and couldn't help herself, she pulled his pants down and started pouring hot wax on him and whipping him with belts and whips and chain. Coyia felted in control and she lifted her skirt up got ready to get on top of him with blood and bruises all over him that made her feel like she was the boss and Coyia got right on him before it went in she woke up. When Coyia Woke up she was sweating all over her body and the sheets was soaking wet. She was hornier than she has ever been and she sat up and said "I'm glad that was only a dream, because damn, I kind of liked that crazy as shit ". She laughed to herself and went and changed her sheets and cover and went to shower to use the shower head, then to get ready for the day. She called her cousin Nikki so they could go get their nails done. When Nikki answered she said "What are you doing today bitch," and Nikki said "nothing much just sitting in the house watching T.V with the kids, why, what's up?" Coyia said "let go get our nails done today"?

Nikki thought about it and said "I would, but I don't have no", and right before she said anything Coyia cut her off and said "i'll pay for both of us, I just don't want to go by myself, pleasessss"? Nikki said "since you put it that way then I'm on my way to come get you now then". They hung the phone up and Nikki got dressed and made her way to Coyia's house.

Before Nikki got to Coyia's house, Coyia cleaned up and grabbed her purse and was about to head to the living room to wait on Nikki. A napkin fill on the floor by coyia's coffee table and she bent down to grab it and saw E's number on it. She picked it up and put it in her purse. When Nikki got to Coyia's house she honked the horn and Coyia came out high siding as usually, "heyyyyy baby"! She got into Nikki's car and Nikki joined in on Coyia's vibe, "ahhhhh shit, let's do this girl"! They both busted out laughing and shook each others hand hand. Nikki drove off and asked what shop they were going too. Coyia said "Let's go to the one place on M.L.K between Alberta and killingsworth," Nikki said "bet," and turned up the music and they sang all the way to the shop. When Coyia and Nikki got there the place was almost full. They had one spot left and Coyia told Nikki to go first and that she wanted her to meet her friend in for Nikki to tell her what she thought about him. Nikki said "okay", and went and got her nails started on.

Coyia grabbed her phone out her purse and the napkin and called E. Coyia had a big smile on her face while she looked out the window and waited for E to answer. E answered the phone "hello", Coyia cleared her throat and said "hey, how are you doing"? E said "I'm doing good M.s Coyia and how about yourself"? Coyia said "How did you know it was me"? E laughed and said "because I don't have a girl and I don't give out my number much, so that means this could have been the only girl that I gave my number to, and to add to that I couldn't stop thinking about your fine ass since we departed from each other that night." That gave Coyia butterflies to her stomach. She didn't know how to take that, but it made her happy. Coyia said "I was wondering what you were doing today," E responded "nothing that I know of, why?" Coyia said "because I want to know if you would like to come to lunch with me in my cousin," E said "yeah, when and where and what time". Coyia said "well we're getting our nails and feet done now but, if you don't mind, you can meet us here at the nail shop". E said "and where is that at?" "it's on M.L.K between Alberta and killingsworth, you know across the street from that big building place whatever it is". E said "I actually know where that is, i'll be there in 20 to 30 minutes". Coyia said "okay see you when you get here". She hung up the phone and someone was just getting up out of the chair. Coyia was sitting next to some older lady that was right in between her and nikki. Coyia asked the older lady if she didn't mind if they talked around her.

The older lady said "baby, I don't mind, she's just about done, then I'm off to get my feet done." Coyia said "I heard that ma'am go on with your bad self", the whole nail shop laughed and Coyia and the older lady slapped hands". Coyia said to Nikki, "Remember that movie I told you to watch," Nikki said "which one," Coyia said "that movie (MISERY), with that crazy white lady breaks that dudes legs". Nikki said "o yeah, that movie was crazy". Coyia said "I know, I was wondering if a sista had did something like that to a brotha, how would that movie turned out. Everyone started laughing and saying funny remarks about what would happen if it was a black man and a black woman in that situation.

Just as Coyia started talking E walked in the door and everyone looked at him and the place got really quiet. Everyone looked around and busted out laughing. E looked at everyone in there and said "Did I walk in at the wrong time or what"? Coyia asked the lady working on her hands to hold on for one second and she stood up and walked toward E. As she got close to him she said out loud for the whole room to hear, "This might be the first one to experience that black misery". Everyone was laughing and screaming in the shop. An older woman yelled to E, "young man you better run"! Coyia smiled as she walked right up to E and said "don't mind them, we are just having girls talk," and E said "I hope so". Coyia told E to sit over in they corner and they were almost done. He did as she asked him to and Coyia went back to her seat to get her nails finished. Nikki said "Is that who you were talking too"? Coyia shook her head and smiled.

Nikki said "not a bad girl", Coyia smiled and said "Thanks, I was hoping to get that from you". The girls finished getting their nails done and started heading toward the door. E opened the door for them and said "so where are we eating lady's", and Coyia said "ooooouuu, how about that soul food place on like 14th and dekum, it's cheap and they have some bomb ass food there". E said "I'm down, so I'll just follow y'all then". Coyia said "yeah", and Nikki coughed and looked at Coyia. Coyia said "o yeah, E this is my cousin Nikki, and Nikki this is E". E stuck his hand out to shake Nikki's hand and she looked at it and said "hhmm do you have a real name E", he laughed and said "yeah, it's Edward, now can I shake your hand", Nikki looked at him and at his hand, then decided to shake his hand. Coyia said "now that we all know each other let's go eat and everyone got in their cars and drove off. They pulled up to the soul food joint and E opened the door for the girls.

They were seated quickly because no one was in there so the waiter waited on them to order. They did a lot of talking, mainly Nikki asking E a 1000 in 1 question. Everything worked out for coyia. Nikki got to meet him and just in case anything happened to her again she knew Nikki knew everything about him now. E paid for everyone's meals and had to leave. so they took the rest of their food to go and went their separate ways. Coyia asked Nikki how she liked him and her responses made Coyia happy. She thought he was a nice person and very handsome but didn't like that he was a hustler because she knew what came with it but never said nothing to Coyia about it cause she was so happy and didn't want her to feel like she was hating on her.

As they drove Coyia was staring out the window and saw a porno store and said to Nikki, "ooouuu, let's go in there nikki", Nikki looked at her and said "why do you want to go in there, girl you need Jesus". Coyia just laughed at her and asked her to turn around and Nikki did as she was asked. When they pulled up to the porn store Nikki gave Coyia a nasty look and Coyia said "bitch dont look at me like that, shit you could find something in here to spice up your boring as married life, with all that missionary shit yall be doing in there", they both busted out laughing and Nikki hit Coyia in the shoulder and said "bitch, my sex life ain't boring, thank you very much, it's just hard finding time to really put it on him with the kids always around". Coyia understood what she meant, and told her, "it was all good". They walked into the store and saw things people only seen in movies. Coyia walked in there like she had been there before and got to looking around and asking questions as if this was just normal things people did. Nikki on the other hand was not feeling it at all.

They walked through the store and Nikki grabbed some weird vibrators and some lubrication with a warming sensation. They walked to the corner and Coyia gave Nikki a dildo and she damn near had a heart attack. Nikki screamed and said "aahhh, stop playing so damn much, shit". Coyia laughed hard and the person from the counter laughed a lot harder because they knew she was unconvertable ever since she walked into the store, and not too many people go in there, so that was a great laugh for the person behind the counter. As they walked up to the counter the cashier rang up their merchandise. The cashier said "45.99." Coyia reached in her purse and gave the guy a 50-dollar bill and told them to keep the rest. Nikki was getting ready to walk out the door when she noticed a box behind the counter and asked the cashier what was in it. The cashier told them that he didn't know, his boss just told them he was getting rid of a lot of stuff from the back and they needed more room for the new stuff that was about to be brought in. Coyia asked the cashier to look inside of the box, but the cashier said "bosses rules is we can't open the box, so what u see is what you get". Nikki said "so everything in those boxes are supposed to be a surprise." The cashier said "right", Coyia asked "How much is this surprise box going for then, since we can't look inside of it," "35 dollars' '.

As Coyia was about to pull some more money out of her wallet she heard a loud noise coming from the front door. "Bitch ass motherfucka, I want my money back, this shit ain't nothing but chains and handcuff, I can't do nothing with this shit," the cashier said "look I told you all sell were final, take that shit and give me a break man, come on, I don't want to call the police, but your really asking for it now, sir, I need you to leave please"!

The guy that came in said "you gotta call them this time, because I'm not leaving until I get my motherfucking money back, so call them, I'll wait"! The cashier grabbed the phone and asked Coyia to hold on for a second. Coyia said "it's okay, i'll just come back for the box", the cashier shook his head at Coyia. She grabbed her bag and started to head toward the door. Coyia walked past the guy with the box in front of him and stopped. For some strange reason she couldn't stop thinking about her dream and having someone tied up to her bed. She turned around and asked "how much did you buy that for sir", the guy looked at Coyia and said "60 dollars" Coyia said "o, will I was going to help you and buy it off you, but thats way too much, he told me 20 dollars up there, and I was trying to help you not go to jail". She started walking towards the door and as soon as she got to the door the guy ran to her and said "okay, okay, I just needed a little more help, but if you want I can go steal some more stuff for you, since I'm 86's and really don't plan on coming back in this area anymore anyways". Coyia said "but, he said all sales were final," the guy said "No, all sales are final when you walk out the door, and you're still in the store". He smiled at Coyia and Coyia walked back to the corner and said, ``can I please get my money back please," the man looked at the door and saw the other guy giggling and walking around the store putting stuff in his backpack. He said "man, I already know what's about to go down, but I don't even care because the police are on their way and I can't touch no one, I just work here". He looked around and said "a man the police will be here in 10 minutes."

As he gave Coyia back her money. The guy walking around said "I might as well get as much as i can since I only got 7 minutes," and he walked through the store just throwing everything's in his bag, and didn't have a care in the world the police would be there in less than 7 minutes now.

Coyia stood at the door cracking up because that wasn't some shit you didn't see every day. She walked out the store and got in the car with Nikki. Nikki started the car and got ready to pull off and Coyia grabbed her hand and said "hold on real quick and looked at the front door".

The man came out of the store with a backpack full of stuff and Coyia told him to hop in and told Nikki to drive down the street fast. When they were a mile or two down the guy poured everything out on the seat and left the surprise box on the floor. Coyia said "damn I really didn't need all of that", the guy said "will I really need the money my bad if I over did it, plus my kids need their cake for their birthday today, so thank you". Coyia handed the guy a sixy dollars for his kids and said thanks and he got out of the car and walked off smiling cause he was now the dad of the year. Nikki pulled off and said "I hope he doesn't get hemmed up by the police before he gets to his kids," Coyia shook her head and said "that part", they both laughed as they headed to Coyia's house. When Coyia got back to the house E called her and asked her if she was busy,

Coyia told him she wasn't and E asked if he could come pick her up and Coyia said yea, and she gave him her address and hung up the phone smiling. Before Coyia left with E she called Nikki and told her she was leaving with E, just so somebody knew who she was with this time. E pulled up to Coyia's house and watched her get into his car smiling. E told her right off the back

"Okay check this out, I gotta handle a couple things real quick then after I'm done we can go to the movies or something is that cool with you." Coyia said "okay, I didn't have anything to do today, but stay home and watch TV". E drove all around hitting licks and making his money while Coyia kept her face in her phone and observed E.

Coyia was amazed at how many people wanted powder and she didn't get why they spent so much money for something so little. Coyia said "do all those people buy that shit, or should I say, that small amount of powder for so much money." E smiled and said "Ain't it a trip", they both laughed and he turned the music on and they drove around getting money. When E finished hitting his licks, he drove straight to the movies and Coyia looked at him and said "I see you keep your word", E smiled and said "what do you want to see", Coyia shook her head and said "whatever you want to see". E said coo, and said "lets go get some snacks first", Coyia said "Ain't there food inside the movie theater? E laughed and said "Just come on", and they walked off across the street. E looked at Coyia and said "I hope

you got your big purse"? Coyia looked at E and said "Why you say that
"? They walked into the Dollar Tree and E walked straight to the candy
section. He grabbed everything he could and throw it in Coyia's purse
and she gave him a look and said "Nigga I don't steal ". E said "what you
want", and Coyia grabbed everything she wanted and gave it to E. E asked
Coyia for her purse and she handed it to him. It was funny because E had
a pocket full of money but still stole all kinds of stuff just for the theater
and coyia. For some reason, seeing E walk out the door with her purse full
of snacks, it kind spiced up her night. It wasn't that he stole even though
he had money, it was the thrill of it all.

They got back to the movie theater and went inside to pick a movie.
E asked Coyia what she wanted to watch. She looked up at all the movies
they were showing and pointed to the new Tupac movie. The woman
behind the counter kept looking at Coyia's bag, because she kept hearing
all kinds of chip bags and anything else that could make a sound. E saw
the girl looking at Coyia and grabbed her purse from her and through his
coat over it. The lady asked E ``Excuse me sir, is there any snacks or any
types of food in her purse. E said "I don't know what you're talking about
and no there's not". Coyia looked at E, because he lied to the lady with a
straight face and didn't even blink. E said "Ms. if you don't mind, I would
really like to get to this movie before it starts, you know, so I can go buy
some snacks and refreshments from this place". Coyia busted out laughing
and walked off. The lady handed E the tickets and he said "thank you",
and walked off with a big smile on his face. E was different and kept her
smiling. E handed Coyia back her purse and walked through the movie
theater looking for the right door.

When they found the right door to go into there was a man standing
there looking a peoples tickets and Coyia got nerves and handed the purse
back to E. E held his head high and walked right up to the guy who was
taking the tickets and said "How you doing sir", he smiled at Coyia and
asked for their tickets. For some reason E thought that it would be funny

to put Coyia's purse on the guy's stand and look through all the snacks for the tickets. Coyia was scared as hell, but couldn't stop laughing at E because she knew he had the ticket in his back pocket. E made sure to make a lot of noise while he acted like he looked for the movie tickets. The guy couldn't help but laugh his self and before E could hand the guy the tickets he just laughed and said "man yall go on ahead, you are a funny guy". E picked the purse up and started laughing hard and grabbed Coyia's hand and they walked inside of the theater. When they found there sits Coyia asked E, "Were you scare that they were going to stop you or kick you out at the dudes counter", E looked at Coyia and put his feet on the sits in front of him and said "If they can't see what's in your bag then they can't stop you, it there policy."

For some strange reason Coyia liked E for taking the purse from her at the door. She knew that was something small, but in her eye's that was something big and it made her like him that much more. They sat close to the wall, because it seemed darker and they wanted to enjoy their snacks without getting caught. They watched the movie and Coyia got comfortable and laid on E's shoulder. He looked at her and I guess she felt his eyes watching her and she looked up only to see his eyes staring right at hers. E kissed Coyia real quick and turned his head back towards the movie screen. Coyia was taken by surprise and didn't know what to do. So she grabbed E chin and turned it toward her and they kissed passionately inside the movie theater. E started rubbing her back and touching her breast. Coyia took her right hand and started playing with his zipper and started to unbutton his pants. She stopped kissing E and went straight for his dick and started suck his dick. E looked around to make sure no one was looking and that the security wasn't walking up and down the aisles. Coyia couldn't do what she wanted to do so she got on her knees and got in front of him. She put her mouth on his dick and then stopped. She looked up and told him to make sure he looks out for the movie people. E shook his head and said "okay", then laid back in his seat and closed his eyes with one hand on the back of Coyia's head. E grabbed the back of Coyia's hair and moved her head how he wanted it. Coyia liked that he showed her how he liked his dick suck, but she had other plans up her sleeves. Coyia took E's dick and deepthroat it. She felt his dick in the back of her throat and she pushed as hard as she could. E looked around to make sure the coast was clear then at Coyia and said "Damn I ain't never seen that before, shit keep doing it." Coyia laughed and said "Maybe another time."

She stood up and looked at all the people in the theater and made sure no one was paying attention and pulled her pants down and sat on his dick. E was surprised and scared at the same time because he didn't have a condom before she sat down and he had never done anything like this in the movie. Coyia rode the fuck outta of his dick until she nutted and then got back on her knees and suck his dick so fast that he nutted all in her mouth and she swallowed every inch of his dick while he came inside of her mouth. She made sure she pushed his dick so far down her throat as she could. She wanted his babies to swim all in her stomach. E grabbed the back of her head and tried to pull her away, but Coyia just pushed down harder and made sure he was satisfied. E grabbed her head with his other arm and started screaming, "aaaahhhh, stop playing, women." Coyia lifted up her head and smiled while she wiped her mouth and said "What are you talking about ", E just smiled and was out of breath. Coyia looked at E and asked him "are you ready for round too"? E was staring at the ceiling and breathing hard and said "hellllll, naw, shit, I'm a sucka for head and you don't play fair shit, you got my feet all hurting from squeezing to tight and shit, fuck no, give me until the rest of this movie and will again k". Coyia just laughed and laid on his shoulder as they watched the rest of the movie together. When the movie was over they walked out of the theater and as they were walking by the restrooms E pulled Coyia inside real quickly. Coyia almost fell over her own feet the way he grabbed her. She saw an older gentleman pissing in looking right at her through the mirror and E just smiled at him and put his fingers to his mouth as he pulled Coyia inside the stall with him and Coyia shut the door behind them. The older man said to them "you two enjoy, you only live once", and E said "I heard that", and pulled his pants down.

Coyia dropped to her knees to get him started again and E grabbed the back of her hair and moved her head how he wanted it to be. After a while of giving him what he wanted E pull Coyia by the hair to stand up and he bent her over the toilet and rammed his dick deep inside her. No condom at all, just a big black dick. Coyia moan loud, the pleasure that she was getting from all the excitement and adrenaline. E was beating her pussy up inside that little stall, people and kids were walking in the restroom and Coyia knew for sure every last one of them heard them inside that stall. Coyia couldn't stop moaning so loud and E kept making her hit her head on the door. Coyia laughed hard and moaned loudly because this was so crazy, and freaky and E was so spontaneous with how he went about everything that Coyia was really excited and that turned her on and made her nut just looking at him. He had her standing up against the door with her ass out. He fucked her hard and harder and she got louder and louder.

That made E happy and he was about to nut, but he pulled out and told Coyia to sit on his dick. She did as she was told and for some apparent reason she got wild with it and louder and E couldn't hold it back, he came and hard. Coyia felt him coming inside her and he loaded her up with nut, because she came with him and right as they were getting that tingling feeling, they heard a voice say "Ma'am you know this is the men's bathroom and you're not supposed to be in here. Coyia's eye popped out her head and she jumped off of E and said "I'm sorry, I just couldn't hold it. I'm leaving now. She pushed herself off of E and pulled her panties up as fast as she could. E stood up quick and pulled his pants up while laughing because they got caught.

They rushed out the stall and saw a young white guy standing there with a movie shirt on. You could tell he worked there. They ran past him with the biggest smile on their face. They ran to the car and got inside and they both looked at the door. The worker had run to the front door and started looking around for their car with a phone to his ear. They both ducked down and E looked at Coyia and said "Have you ever done something like this before," Coyia said "no, not at all", and they busted out laughing and waited for the guy to go back into the theater. E started the car and drove Coyia home and when they got there he looked Coyia in her eyes and grabbed her and pulled her to him and gave her a very deep passionate kiss and said to her "I have to pick up some money, but i'll be here tomorrow to pick you up around 3 o'clock so be ready. Coyia had butterflies swimming all around in her stomach. She thought to herself, that this time could actually be the real thing. She didn't want E to leave, but she didn't want whatever they had to end. Coyia didn't want things ending like the last few dates she had. So Coyia kissed E one last time and told him that she would be waiting by the phone for his call at 3 tomorrow. Coyia got out of the car and made sure she switched her hips as hard as she could. She walked halfway to her door and looked back just to see if E was watching, and he was, and that made her smile. she felt wanted, something she has been wanting for a long time. She walked into her house and locked the door and jumped straight into her bed. She didn't want to wash off E scent. Coyia prayed to God that night to make sure that he was the one to marry her and she fell asleep hoping to dream about him.

Weeks went by with the two love birds and everything felt great for the most part. E started feeling some kind of way because Coyia always wanted to go with him on his runs. Coyia thought differently, she worked a lot as well and felt like they didn't spend enough time with each other, and that he always messed up their time together hustling, and leaving her for hours on in. So Coyia decided to just stay with him whenever they spent their time together so that she got all of him. Now E on the other hand wasn't used to that. Always being with his girl 24/7 and no breaks, or at least it felt that way. He still had his side pieces to get at and other bitches always blowing him up so this wasn't working for him. Coyia heard his phone buzzing and she looked at E and said "yo phone is ringing." E looked down at his phone and saw that big booty Stacy was calling. He bites down on his teeth hard and puts his phone back on his lap. Coyia knew it was one of his bitches that he thought she didn't know about, but she did. Coyia went through his phone one night while E was drunk. He came into her house and passed out on the couch. Coyia knew she was wrong for doing it, but she wasn't trying to be noisy, she just thought it was a customer trying to get something. She answered just to let them know that he was done for the night. So she let the phone ring a couple of times while she put E in her bed then went to get his stuff and ended up answering his phone. So after that day, she just stayed with him as much as she could, hoping to see the bitch named Stacy.

Coyia never told E about that night, but she had big plans for that girl, when she seen her, and was hoping to see her soon. Crazy thing about it, is that E knew that Coyia knew he was talking to other females, and that she answered his phone that night because he had seen Stacy that night and planned on meeting up with her later on that night, but he got drunk to soon and ended up leaving the club with his homeboy TC. TC was the only person who knew where Coyia lived because that was the only person E trusted with his life. E woke up at Coyia's that morning and looked through his phone only to see that he had talked to Stacy on the phone, and he knew that he didn't answer the phone, because he would have just popped up at stacy's house. That morning he had asked Coyia what time did he come to her house and she told him around 230, but the call was answered around 3:30 in the morning and that told him all he needed to know.

Coyia was staring a E and asked him "why he didn't answer the phone"? E told her "because it was the same person that was calling already just trying to see where he was". Coyia rolled her eyes and said "okay", and laughed. She looked at E and said "look, Imma tell you like this if anyone of them bitches even think about touching you, talking to you, or even thinking about you coming over and fucking, it's going to be problem, just know that, okay ERIC"! E laughed and said "man you trippin," and he shook his head and kept on driving. E phoned bussed again and Coyia seen his phone flashing this time and yell at E throgh the music, "yo phone is ringing again, and you better answer it this time or I will"! E laughed and turned the music down and looked at his phone to see who was calling. He put his phone down and looked at Coyia and she reached for his phone and answer it, E busted out laughing and said "Man stop playing and give me my phone," Coyia put her hand up to and answer his phone in a mean tone, "HELLO, WHO IS THIS," Tc said "damn Coyia, did the nigga piss you off or something or did I call at the wrong time"? Coyia said "naw this man fucking with me, and I thought you was one of his stank ass bitches that think im not going to beat there ass"! Tc started laughing and said "Man yall need to cut that out, with yall love bird asses, but look I was trying to see if yall was trying to come to this party on 141ᵗʰ and fremont"? Coyia asked "Who's party is it?" Anthony said "my homeboy ricks party at his house, E know where it is." Coyia looked at E and asked him if he wanted to go to the party and E told her "yep let's go change and tell him we're on our way". She told Tc everything E said and hung up the phone. They went to Coyia house to get dressed and headed to the party. Coyia did her make-up in the car on the way to the party.

E couldn't help but watch her, because of what she was wearing, it made his dick hard. When they got to the party, they saw so many cars and E knew it was cracking. They walked into the party together from the side of the house. E was like a celebrity. Everybody ran up to him and shook his hand and gave him some type of love. E had the biggest smile on his face while he held onto Coyia's arm and got love from everyone. When they finally got all the way to the backyard they saw women in two piece swimsuits and brothers in shorts walking around. They saw people in the swimming pools splashing and having a good time. They saw people shooting dice on one end of the house and card games in the middle.

People were playing tunk, spades, dominos and everyone had a big plate of food in front of them. They drank liquor for days and their music was on point. Tc walked up to E and gave both him and Coyia some love. Tc told Coyia and E that he was happy to see them and pointed them to the domino's table. That was another thing Coyia really didn't like about E. He was a gambler and this party here was a gambler's dream house. Coyia kissed E on his lips and asked him if he wanted something to eat.

He shook his head and told her he wanted everything and they walked off. When Coyia got their food together and got to the table where E was, she sat his plate down and stood over him eating because there was nowhere to sit down. She didn't have much on her plate, so when she did finish she put her plate under his plate and watched E play domino's. Coyia had one hand on E's shoulders and the other one on her phone. She was watching a Facebook newsfeed. When she heard a voice that sounded familiar and looked around for where it was coming from. As she looked through the crowd she saw everyone walking to the side of the house, so Coyia looked back at her phone, and then she heard Rell's voice and looked up because Ant said "chingy we got drinks for days". Coyia tensed up and she squeezed her phone and E shoulder. E looked up and said "Damn baby, why the fuck are you squeezing my shoulder like that shit"? E looked up at Coyia only to see her crying. He jumped out of his seat and said her name "Coyia"? she was in another world so E yelled her name "COYIA"? she snapped out of whatever she was in and looked at E and he asked her "whats wrong baby"? Coyia said "Remember, I told you about that dude that raped me" he shook his head and Coyia pointed to where Ant and Rell was. He looked over to where she was pointing and said "Those are the nigga's right there"? Coyia said "Yes," in a low voice. E grabbed her shoulder and said "Coyia are you sure it was those nigga's right there"? She yelled "Yes I'm sure"! E looked at Tc and said "you ready"? Tc said "nigga, I been waiting for a reason to fuck those nigga's up in she just gave me a good reason to, let's make this shit happen".

They got up from the table and the other two guy did as will. They didn't know what was going on but they had E and Ants back because E and Ant was some cool ass dude's so they had their backs. E walked right over to where the crowd was and yell "Ant in that weak as nigga chingy", everyone looked at E walking to them and Ant said "aint nothing weak over here bitch ass nigga", E said "you see that girl over there", and everyone looked at where E was pointing to and they all saw Coyia standing up balling. Ant and chingy looked and saw Coyia and before they could say anything E punch Ant right in the face in chingy hit E from the side. E's homeboy Tc fired on chingy and from that point on everything turned into a big brawl. Tables was turned over and people were throwing glasses and chair all around the back yall. You heard females yelling at the top of their lungs and with all the noise that was happening that made the man of the house come out and he got mad at what he had just saw. So he said "okay nigga's don't want to respect my shit then watch this and went back into the house madder than a mothafucka. people from the side lines that was watching was placing bets on who would win between certain people that they thought was a good match. From someone that was watching it seem like everyone in the party was fight but a few. The man of the house stuck his head out the window with his SKS and shot it a couple of times and said "Now get yall ungrateful ass out my house and don't ever come back to my shit, if you aint gone by the time I come down stairs, you're a dead man"! Everyone that was fighting took off running, but a few that was beat up bad or knocked out. Coyia was standing in the same spot with a butter knife in one hand and a folk and the other. When everyone took off running she saw E yelling and ran to him. She seen Ant laying on the ground knocked out snoring and it looked like his teeth was missing and she looked at him and started stomping on his head and spitting on him and yelling at him "bitch ass nigga, I hate you for what you done to me", E grabbed her leg and said "Babe, fuck that nigga, I'm laying here stabbed," she turn and said "O my god, sorry baby". Coyia bent down and grabbed

74

E's wound and said "What happen", E said "that bitch ass nigga stabbed me, get me in the house before the police come".

Coyia helped E up and kicked Ant in his mouth and said "bitch ass nigga, and that's for my man", E grabbed her and said "Don't kill him, shit, fuck that weak ass nigga, lets go, im hurting, shit", Coyia threw the knife she had at Ant's chest and it bounced off his chest and she threw the folk she had at his head and said "He needs to die for what he did to me and the folk did the same thing that the knife did and that pissed her off, but she had to get E in the house so she put E arm around her shoulder and walked E into the house. Coyia walked E to the couch and ran back into the kitchen to get paper towels and clean wet rags. She ran back into the living room and started wiping the blood off his skin. While she was doing that the man over the house came downstairs with his SKS in one hand and saw Coyia cleaning someone's wound he said "A bitch take that nigga to the hospital"! and walked around the couch to see his homeboy E and said "O shit nigga I didn't know that was you, and what the fuck happen my nigga"? E looked up and said "That weak ass nigga stabbed me".

The guy kept trying to talk to E while Coyia was trying to talk to him at the same time and Coyia's blood started to boil and she said "Aaaa, can you be quit and go get use something to clean his wound with before my nigga die on your couch, please and what is yo name"? The guy said "My bad, I'm city." Coyia asked City if he had any type of disinfected to clean E wounds. City thought for a second and ran upstairs. Coyia and E heard a lot of noises coming from the stairs. City was moving so fast that he forgot that he moved everything from his bathroom to the kitchen because he knew there was going to be something that went down today, but he forgot that he did that and he tore his bathroom up looking for his first aid kit. He ran to the top of the stairs and yelled, "I ain't got shit in here, my bad y'all we got to run him to the hospital or something". Coyia said "Baby please let's just go to the hospital, please"! E said hell naw, I still got that punk ass warrant hanging over my head and I ain't ready to turn myself in, babe just go to the store real quick, it's only right down the street from here, I should be okay until you get back". Coyia said "okay, give me your keys," and E reached in his pocket in pain and said "I don't have them, they must be in the back yard go look for them," and E looked at his boy city and asked him to go with her to make sure that nigga didnt wake up and beat her ass.

City shook his head and followed behind Coyia. Coyia flipped the table that they were playing. on over and looked all around and she saw his keys a few feet away from the table. Coyia grabbed his keys and stepped on Ant's snoring body and kept on running as fast as she could to E's car. As she ran out of the back fence she saw about 2 or 3 girl walking back in where she was running out of and one of the girls asked Coyia ``Hey, was there a Gucci purse back there ", Coyia yelled "I don't know", and she kept running to E's car and sped off to the store.

When Coyia left city started walking into the house and heard females voice coming from the side of the house. He yell at them before he saw who it was and said "party is over, everyone needs to leave." One of the girls said "we know, but my home girl left her purse and they appeared from the side of the house and city said "o, my bad Angel." She said it's cool, I'm just looking for my shit and we gone bro, sorry about your party, but that shit was crackin 'tho". The other girls said "Right", and city said "Go ahead and look for yo stuff. City stood over ant body and poured water on him and told him to leave, I gotta go in here my homeboy got stabbed," and he walked in the house. One of the girls walked to the back door and saw E sitting there with blood all over him and said "Stacy, ain't that yo dude E", Stacy walked to the back door with a curious look on her face and she ran inside the house and said "Baby, what happened, are you okay"? City and E looked up and E said "I'm coo babe, that weak ass nigga stabbed me." Stacy worked at the hospital and saw stuff like this all the time. She told city to move out the way and said "let me see it, I'm a nurse". City moved out the way and Stacy asked him for a knife or some scissors. City ran upstairs back to his bathroom and saw the scissors sitting on the counter and ran as fast as he could back to Stacy. He handed them to her and she cut his shirt off. She told city to give her some alcohol or something to clean his wound with.

He ran to the kitchen and found his first aid kit and said "Damn, I forgot I put this shit down here", and he ran back to stacy. She cleaned her hands with the alcohol and poured a lot of it on his wounds and E yelled loudly. She saw rags and paper towels sitting on the floor and pour more alcohol on it and wiped away the blood and looked at his wound. She said "It ain't that bad, he didn't stab you to bad to hit an artery, but you will need stitches." Stacy looked inside the first aid kit and saw a needle and thread and was about to sow E up but he stopped her and said "Hold on"! He looked at the city and asked him for some pain pills or some drunk or something before she stuck that needle in him. City thought about it for a second and said "my nigga the best I can do is some strong as druck because I don't pop pills", E looked at city strange and said "fuck it, shoot it", and city ran to the kitchen and grabbed the ever clear and gave it to E to drink. Stacy started sowing E up after 4 big cups and boy did it hurt without pain medicine. Stacy knew he was there with his girl but she played her part and watched E from the shadows. E saw Stacy there and they made eye contact but he gave a head nod to her letting her know that he was with Coyia and she nodded back and smiled. Stacy saw her run out the house and decided to make her move. She stood over E after she was done stitching him up and said "All done daddy", he smiled and said "damn that alcohol is catching up to me, shit".

Stacy bent down and hugged him and asked "Who did this to you daddy, I swear Imma make whoever suffer". E told her not to worry about it, and that he already handled it. Stacy kissed E's neck and for some reason that kiss went down from his neck and down to his dick.

Stacy smelled really good for some reason and the pain E was just in went away all of sudden or it didnt hurt to bad now. E rolled his neck so

Stacy could kiss his neck better and everyone stood around watching. Stacy stopped kissing his neck and looked around after she heard her home girl say "ooouuu." Stacy asked everyone to give them a second to themselves for a minute or two.

Everyone walked to another room but city. City walked up to E other ear and said "Bro, don't forget about your girl that went to the store". E said "Yep, good lookin bro look out for me". City said "I'm about to go to the back and make sure everything is everything real quick". City walked into the other room and got everyone walked to the back yard cleaned up and put it back together real fast. Stacy took off her coat and pulled down E's pants and started sucking his dick.

E was so drunk that he didn't even think about Coyia even after his homeboy told him that she just ran to the store right down the street. E said Stacy "what are you doing man"? she said "What you want me to do", E said "man who said I wanted this"? She pulled his dick out and said "him while she stared at his dick, that was in full attention. She sucked the shit out of his dick, and the alcohol played a big part. She sucks his dick better than she ever did before and she made sure that he was loving it. She would go fast then slow, then she would put his whole dick inside her mouth and start humming and pull out humming. She spits on it and jacked it off until she felt him moving with her. While she was sucking his dick she was taking off her pants with her other hand and when everything was off she jumped up and sat on his dick before he could even open his eyes. E was bussing from the ever clear that he didn't even care and Stacy rode the shit out of him. She knew if she would have gotten up that he might have stopped her so she turned her body around while she was still sitting on him. Little by little and when she was facing him and she looked at him and saw his face she squirted all over him. Stacy started kissing E passionately and he pushed her off of him and told her to stand up. She did as she was told and stood up and bent over the couch. and E rammed his dick inside of her and pulled her hair and thrusted inside of her hard.

Coyia was flying through traffic to help her man. Coyia ran every red light she passed and almost hit people walking across the street in the cross walks. When she pulled up to the wal-mart she parked right in front of the store and kept the car on and ran inside of the store as fast as she could. She saw a worker walking towards her and she asked her where the medicines aisle is? The lady said "Sorry ma'am I just started today", and Coyia took off running. She ran to a clerk who was ringing people up and pushed past everyone and asked her as fast as she could in a heavy breathing way. "Where is the medicine aisle at," the lady said, "Give me a second this lady was first," Coyia screamed at the top of her lung "bitch where is the fucking medicine aisle at bitch it's an emergency", the lady pointed her to the aisle and said "some people are just rude nowadays", and kept on ringing people up. Coyia ran as fast as she could to where the rude lady had pointed her to and she grabbed as much as she could hold and ran out the store without paying for anything. She threw everything on the seat and drove off. As Coyia was driving back to City's house she started praying that E was okay and that he wouldn't die on her today.

City and the girls that were in the backyard were done cleaning and they had been drinking and wanted to use the bathroom. The only problem with that was that the bathroom was upstairs and they had to walk past E in Stacy. City told them to be quiet and follow him inside.

They shook their heads and followed behind city. They saw Stacy with her head on the couch and E hitting it from the back. E looked up and city pointed upstairs and E shock his head and kept on fucking Stacy while looking at her homegirls. They blew kisses to E and ran up the stairs quietly. When the girls got done using the bathroom they went into city guest room and finished their drinks and smoked their cigarettes and city rolled up some weed for them to smoke.

When Coyia got back to the house and she ran into the fence the same way she went out of it. As she was running in the backyard she heard women laughing and she slowed down and hoped E was okay. She got all the way to the backyard and didn't see anyone. She looked up and saw smoke coming from the window and someone spit out the window and Coyia flew in the house to make sure E wasn't dead.

After city and the girls went upstairs he made Stacy get back on her knees to finish him off. Stacy got on her knees and was more than happy to do it. She sucked E dick like she first did when they first started fucking. E brain was telling him something, but his dick was saying something else, and Stacy wasn't helping at all. E put his hand on the back of her head and grabbed her hair and moved her head exactly how he wanted her to move. For some reason the hairs on the back of E's neck stood up and something didn't feel right. E had his eyes closed, but opened them because something didn't feel right. As he opened his eyes he looked downed to see Stacy sucking his dick like a crazy woman and he was about to nut all in her mouth. He started to nut, when he heard something on the side of him fall and hit the ground hard. Coyia was standing there and E had forgotten everything had happened to him that ever clear had him in another world and his boy was supposed to let him know when she got back. when E look to see what had fell he didn't see anything or anyone there. So he turns back to Stacy and told her he was about to nut. Coyia was about to kill the both of them and went to find something to make that happen. She looked around and didn't see anything. so she grabbed a bottle of liquor and a roller to make pizza dough with. E was nutting all in Stacy mouth and she was taking every bit of it.

For some reason E looked back over toward the kitchen and remember that Coyia had went to the store to get his stuff to fix him up and he seen the bandages and alcohol stuff on the ground and said "Oh shit, move," and he tried to pull Stacy off him and she didn't move as he tried to get up, that's when Coyia came out and cracked E on the top of his head and busted the bottle over Stacy head. They were both knock out cold. All Coyia could do was cry and run out of the house after saying "I ran out this bitch, to help your ass, and this is what I come back to bitch, we're done". Everyone heard the glass break, but they thought it was E and Stacy. Which it was but they were knocked out cold down the stairs bloody and slept. Coyia ran out of the back yard and jumped into E car and drove herself home.

When she got there she left the keys in the car and went into the house crying. When she got into her room her phone rang and she looked at it only to see E calling but she didn't answer. She got a text shortly after that read "Baby, I'm sorry, I swear that was the drank and that bitch tricked me, please answer"? Coyia just sat the phone down and another text came saying "baby, I plan on making you my wife, please answer"? E had sent another text with a wedding ring that was the most beautiful thing Coyia had seen but her heart and mind told her no cause he wasn't worth it. She turned her phone off and cried. She turned the TV on only to see the movie she had paused and she played the movie and cried herself to sleep. For some reason Coyia had a dream about being with a man that had everything in life and was good to her. When she woke up she got mad because everything rushed back to her like that shit with E had just happened. She looked at the TV and saw that her movie had stopped and she started it over and yelled out loud. "Why the fuck can't I find a good a man, shit, every nigga nowadays is for themselves and now, Imma stealing love, fuck it". I'm done with these weak ass cheating ass, lying ass, stealing yo pride dignity ass, punks". I don't want no pimps, players, cheating ass men, these men are breaking us down and don't want nothing in life, but to get a head alone. So I guess I need to take matters into my own hands and I swear I'm on this misery shit, I'm going to go get mine now, since they're out there hiding.

Coyia took her sleeping medication and went back to sleep. Tomorrow was going to be a good day for her and she couldn't wait. When Coyia woke up in the morning the first thing she did was order another bed from rent a center that had a long metal post on each side of her bed.

When the people from rent a center were done, Coyia got in the shower and put on her sweats and treated herself to the spa. She took a mud bath for a few hours and got all waxed up from her face on down. She got her nails and feet done and enjoyed a wonderful massage. When she got done with her relaxing time at the spa Coyia decided to go to the mall for a new dress. She stopped by Victoria Secret for some bomb ass lingerie and went to forever 21 for a dress. Coyia looked all around for the perfect dress but couldn't find any. As she was heading to the door she saw someone returning an all black dress with a slit in the leg part and enough to see her breast perfectly. Coyia walked up to the woman who was returning it and said "I'll pay you a hundred dollars for that dress right now. The dress was only 20 dollars on sale, but she didn't care. Coyia had the money and was going all out today. The woman snatched the dress back from the teller and said "Shit, here you go". Coyia and the teller laughed and everyone left happy. When Coyia got back home she lotioned herself down and put on her most expensive perfume. She put her dress on and then put her makeup on. She got her diamond earrings and flat ironed her hair.

When she was finished putting herself together she walked out the house smiling and ready to find her a man. Coyia drove around for a while looking for the perfect place to find a good man.

As she drove she thought about every possible way that she could get someone to her house. First she thought about drugging them, then she realized that she didn't have anything to drug them with. Then she thought about hitting them over the head with something, but figured that she would have to put them in her drink alone and she was going for that. She thought about every movie that she had ever seen and said "You know what this shit might not be for me, shit I ain't with all that shit". She pulled into a bar near the airport called the landed spot. It was a strip club, but she figures that people would get off the plane and go straight there from the airport.

When she walked inside, it was packed. Coyia walk straight to the bar and order a sex on the beach. She looked around and saw everyone that wasn't either with a woman or looking at a woman looking at her and she just turned to the bar and looked at everyone through the mirror.

There were a lot of men in there and it seemed like only kids kept coming up to her on some kid shit or talking that pimp shit and she shut that down right away. She sat in that club for hours sipping on her drink and she had had enough and started to walk out the door.

As she was walking out and reach to open the door someone opened the door. Coyia stopped in her tracks. Damn, you must have had a rough day or a tough week if you're wearing that, that's a me time dress. Coyia looked him up and down and smiled because he was so right.

Coyia saw that his pants were all the way pulled up and he was well dressed with beautiful white teeth and wasn't too flashy with his gold that he had on. The guy said, "You leaving so early Ms.", as he held his hand out. Coyia grabbed his hand and said "Coyia, and there nothing in here for me, it's only kids in here and I'm done with trying to be somebody mama", the guy laughed and Coyia said "I didn't catch your name"? He said "Devon, but everyone calls me Dedee". Coyia felt good about this. Dedee asked Coyia to come back inside and have a drink with him. She agreed and for some reason everything she was thinking before she got to the bar had slipped out of her mind or it must've been the drinks she had before dedee came in. They talked for hours and got to know each other and Dedee paid for everything. That made Coyia feel good. After talking Coyia started getting in her feelings and started crying and just fell into Dedee's arm. All he did was hold her and listen to her talk. Coyia felt safe in his arms and when she realized that she was in his arms she pulled herself together and apologized for messing up the mood. As she wiped the tears from her eye's with her hands Dedee handed her some napkins and as Coyia reached for them they made eye contact and when she looked in his eyes she saw love and kindness and warmth and she wanted that. Coyia saw a man walking toward them and she stared at him hard. Dedee saw Coyia staring and turned to see what she was looking at and saw his homeboy curty walking up to him. His homeboy asked "a man, you ready to go, shit I lost all my money on that punk as poker machine."

Dedee looked at Coyia and introduced his friend to Coyia. "Coyia, this is man curty, curty this is Coyia," they shook hands and said hi to each other. Dedee gave curty some money to go order a drink asked him to give them 5 more minutes. Dedee asked Coyia if she wanted another drink and this time she was mad because his friend had to fuck up a perfect night. So she said "Yes I want an A.M.F this time", and he order the same. Coyia asked if he had to take his friend home. Dedee told her no that he was riding with him and that his car was at curty house.

Coyia understood and really didn't want the night to end. So she offers to take Dedee home if that was fine and he agreed. When curty finished his drink he walked back up to Dedee and Coyia and said "bro you ready, I'm not trying to be rude but everyone has left and yall act like yall dont see that", they both looked around and started laughing. Dedee told curty that he was going to ride with Coyia and curty said "Coo, I didn't want to take yo ass all the way home anyways, And you miss pretty thing, the next time I see you, you better have a bomb ass friend with you or a sexy ass mama for my sexy ass." Coyia, Dedee, and curty busted out laughing and Coyia shook her head and said okay. Curty and Dedee shook hands and curty left. Coyia finish her drink and was ready to go as well. Coyia was drunk when she stood up and the world started spinning. Dedee grabbed her just before she fell and said "Maybe I should drive". Coyia smiled and handed him the keys. She told him where she lived and told him that he had to stay the night.

Coyia fell asleep in the car on the way home and Dedee woke her up when he got on her street and she pointed to her house. He parked in front of her house and helped Coyia get out the car and walked her inside of the house. Coyia told him that he could either sleep in the front room or in her room. Dedee told her that he would sleep on the couch and she walked to the hallway closet to get him a blanket and a pillow. While she walked down the hall Dedee got up and looked around Coyias house. Sex artifacts and sex pictures where everywhere. There was incense and candles everywhere. She even had sex movies just sitting out like it was the thing to do. He walked toward the hallway to see her photos that were on her wall. It looked like she really knew how to have a good time.

Coyia walked up to Dedee and handed him his blanket and pillow. She saw that he was staring at Nikki and she said "That's me in my cousin Nikki, we were fucked up in that photo,"

Dedee looked at a few more and said "It looked like you were fucked up in all your photos," Coyia just busted out laughing. She had to use the restroom and excused herself. Dedee went to the couch and laid the cover and pillow down how he wanted it and heard Coyia coming toward him. He sat down and looked up and saw that all she had on was a robe. Coyia walked to the movies and asked him "what do you want to watch," Dedee replied "I don't care," and she just turned the t.v on only to see that the last movie she was watching was in pause on the t.v screen.

She looked back at Dedee and said my bad, I was watching something before I left and went to the bar. I was bored and needed a drink. She said "matter of fact do you want a drink", Dedee said "naw", he had to work in the morning and Coyia dropped to her knees and begged him "please have one drink with me"? Dedee looked at Coyia and said "What, you still want to drink and you almost fell on your face tonight". Coyia looked up at Dedee with his sexy ass eye's and said "just a little, please", Dedee felt like Coyia was coming on too strong and didn't know if it was the alcohol or if that's just how she was. So he went alone with it and took a deep breath and said "women I have to work tomorrow and I have a very important meeting so I need you to have some mouthwash and I need to be home early", "okay". She put her right hand in the air and said "I swear, I will be up before you, so is that a yes' '. He didn't want to seem rude, and for damn sure wasn't ready to be put out this late at night kick it shit, so he agreed. Coyia jumped up and ran to the kitchen to make the drinks.

and it felt like cupid had just shot Coyia with a love arrow, because at that very moment she fell in love with Dedee on sight and was willing to go to extra lengths to show him. Coyia took bits and pieces of his food and really just watched Dedee eat. When he was finished with his food, Coyia jumped up and tried to grab his plate. Dedee looked at Coyia, but wouldn't let the plate go. He said "I can wash my own plate." Coyia started laughing in replied "Not in this house you won't, thats a women job to cater to her man and guess especially after a long day of work, naw don't sweat it I got it." Dedee wouldn't not let the plate go, and said "The way I was raise, whoever cooked the food didn't have to clean anything thing, but everyone else had to clean up after the cook especially after cooking a big meal like this".

Coyia melted inside all she did was smile and a great pause was heard for a few seconds and Coyia said "Aaaawwww that was cute, but my house, my rules and right now your still a guess and my man won't be doing any cleaning around this house now let it go". He thought he heard her say her man, but did not sweat it and he let go of the plate. Coyia walked the plates into the kitchen and while she was walking back to the room she stopped in the bathroom and touch up on her smell goods. She sprayed some body spray her body and rubbed her body down ass fast as she could with baby lotion. She knew actually what she was doing and she wanted to fuck the shit outta Dedee. She walked into the room and turned the lights out and walked right in front of the t.v and started undressing. She did it like she was the only one in the room. Dedee watched her strip naked right in front of him and his little soldier stood right up. He couldn't help it, her body was so beautiful, he said "you have a marvelous body Coyia." Coyia glanced up and seen Dedee dick stand straight up and she smiled. She went to the other side of the bed and got in the covers. She scooted all the way over to Dedee and cuddle up next to him. Dedee opened his arm so Coyia could lay on his chest.

They laid there for a second holding each other. Coyia started rubbing his chest over and over again with her fingers and Dedee knew what that mint. His plan wasn't to fuck that night but she had given him that strong drink and the food top it off. So he grabbed the remote controller and turned the T.V off and turned to Coyia and kissed her on the forehead. She turned over to her back and with her right arm she grabbed his dick and started playing with it. From that point on he knew what it was going to be and knew if it was this easy then he didn't want her but he knew the alcohol was playing a big part as well, but that wouldn't stop him from enjoying that moment with her. He kissed on her neck and ears and whenever he got close to her neck he made sure that his hot breath got to the back of her neck before his lips did. He felt Coyia quiver and she jacked him off faster every time he did that to her neck. She started playing with herself and boy was she wet. Dedee hands was on her breast and rubbing the sides of her body, slowly, barely touching her and getting her to twitch and jerk. that turned him on, but nothing turned him on more than when Coyia couldn't take it no more and she grabbed Dedee's hand and put it right in between her legs and boy was it wet. Dedee dick grew at least 3 more inches after feeling how wet she was. He sucked on her breast and played with her sweet spot until he heard her moan heavily and her legs started to squeeze tightly on his hand. She let out a little orgasm. Dedee thought about going down on her but, by the way things were going he was cool. He had just met her but the way the vibe was going he didn't care, but he had most self-respect for himself. He kissed her stomach as if he was going to go down on her then bit on her legs and kissed her inner thighs. He was a big tease.

Coyia closed her eyes because she thought that he was going to go down on her and the closer he got to her sweet spot the wetter she got. Dedee made his way back up to Coyia's stomach and as he slowly started climbing higher toward her face Coyia's eyes got big and she stared at Dedee with a crazy looked. She was think all kinds of thought, "Why did he stop, no baby please don't stop, it's all your, fuck man, fuck man, damn, he might want me to go down first, will watch this then". Coyia started kissing Dedee and slowly started turning him around. They kissed passionately and long, Coyia felt the chills going down her spine and that made everything feel like this was supposed to be happening. She felt Dedee finger inside of her and he finger the hell out of her while they kissed. Coyia grabbed Dedee hand and pulled it away from her and pinned his hands down to the bed. She slowly kissed his neck and nibbled on his ears while she held his hands. She went down his body kissing every inch of what god had blessed him with and worked her way to her new magic stick. When she got to it she held it in her hands and imagined that it was a magic stick in her hand. She was about to cast a spell on this man with the magic she was about to hit him with after she got done. Coyia sucked his dick and stared at Dedee through the dark. She felt his eye's staring at her and she inmaged him staring back at her. Every now in a then she would stop and feel behind her to make sure no one was behind her then she would look into the dark to make sure she didn't see anyone in the room with them. She would grab his dick tightly to make sure nobody switch like Ant and Rell did.

After a while she figures that she was okay and enjoyed the night with her future husband. Coyia thought to herself "I know he is clean and if he ain't we gonna have a problem because he aint getting rid of me so easily", and Coyia rushed on top of Dedee and sat on his dick. He tried to push her off but with all the alcohol and the feeling he couldn't or didn't want to. He kept his hands on her waist because he wanted to put on a rubber but the feeling was too good and with all her juices flowing on him was crazy and he loved it. He thrusted inside of her deeper and harder. Coyia moaned loudly screaming "Yes daddy, ooooo, my goodness don't stop", Coyia grabbed Dedee's hand and made him grab her hair and she started playing with her breast.

Coyia looked up at the ceiling and rode the shit outta Dedee. She felted her orgasm coming on and laid down on Dedee and sucked his neck hard and long everytime she started to feel her body start to shake. Dedee knew what she was doing and he also knew he had more hickeys than ever. So he decides to take charge and he grabbed Coyia and stood up with her. He grabbed her ass with both hands firmly and picked her up off the bed. He bounced her as high as he could and smiled because she held on for dear life. After doing that position for about ten minutes he laid her down on the bed and made love for a split second. He made sure he went inside of her slowly and smoothly, then he kissed her passionately and turned her around and his dick made its way inside of her from behind. He rammed it inside of her until she nutted hard on him and she couldn't take it anymore and she rolled away from him and looked at Dedee and tried to catch her breath. She said "let me ride you, your wearing me out". They laughed and switched positions and Coyia got back on top of Dedee as he laid on the bed on his back. Coyia rode Dedee slowly and fast all at the same time. she bounced up in down and squirted on him, time after time, she nutted more times then she could count. Dedee started feeling his nut coming and started letting Coyia know in a low voice, but Coyia felt a big one coming and she laid on him, and he knew she was coming but he was too late. He tried his best to get her off him but he was nutting at the same time and he fell into temptation. Coyia knew Dedee was mad and just laid on his chest and apologised because she knew he didn't want to nut inside of her, but Dedee knew he was going home tomorrow and he had to get ready for work. So he plans on going to the hospital tomorrow after work. He grabbed Coyia and laid her on his chest and held her.

Dedee thought to himself this might be the last time I ever see her again so I might as well make the best of this and finish tonight strong since she brought me here to her house and I left my car at my homies house. Coyia got tired and took a long deep breath and went to sleep while Dedee held her.

Dedee woke up to his alarm and Coyia's phone going off. Coyia's woke up startled and jumped out of bed. He was angry because he had a very important meeting to be at and now he was late. Coyia jumped up and went in got his clothes out of the dryer and handed them to him.

Dedee sat on the bed naked with his head down and his face facing to ground as he talked to his boss. Coyia could hear them talking and by the look on Dedee face it wasn't pretty. Coyia could hear his bosses voice through the phone telling him not to come in today and that look on Dedee face was very troubling. Dedee got up and started putting on his clothes and Shacoyia heard his boss tell him not to come in today. She looked puzzle and asked "why are you putting on your clothes on," Dedee was looking at Coyia and said "because of you I missed my important meeting and I missed my raise. I need to get up out of here because I'm mad at myself for even getting to fucked up in the first place". Coyia looked at Dedee and said "So what are you about to do because I heard your boss tell you that you didn't have to come in to work today", he stopped dressing and looked at her with death in his eyes. Coyia already knew what he wanted to say, but he just stared at her. Coyia said "I apologize for not hearing my alarm and not waking you up on time I should have gotten up but, to be honest with you I haven't had this much sleep in a long time and I honestly really never heard your phone or mine, and I'm sorry for that."

Dedee put his clothes on and Coyia asked him if there was anything that she could do to help him or make him feel a little better. Dedee looked at Coyia with a cold stare and said "no, I don't need anything but a ride home". Coyia asked him "if there was any chance that they could meet up again", and Dedee shock his head and said "naw, we ain't right for each other, I mean I enjoyed our night but I mess up a lot that can't be replaced and I don't want to take anything out on you because it was my fault for not handling my business like I was supposed too". Coyia felt hurt because she knew that it was her fault for not waking up like she was supposed to and she messed up alot of things for Dedee. He got dressed and bent down to put his shoes on and Coyia rolled of the bed and grabbed on to Dedee's shoulders and said "can you please think about coming back over because I feel like your my soulmate, it might be to soon but I know that I love you and I don't even know you yet. Please give us a try and let me show you that what I'm saying is true and that my words don't go in one ear in out the other". Dedee stood up and turned his back to her and said, "How could I want someone like you, you drink entirely to much and you are a sex addicted, you think you love me and you just met me and that shit is what a crazy person would say and that's the type of shit that's crazy to me about you".

The crazy part about this was that Dedee was just mad, he missed everything he had to do and if Coyia would have known this she would have just let him leave and she would have given him time to think, but they didn't know each other and Dedee was saying some hurtful shit. So Coyia turned the other way and started crying because she knew he felt the same way about her that she felt for him. she started to see red and she started thinking of all the men that had done her wrong. Everyone that did something to her in the last year and that hurt her heart and she felt ashamed. She was really mad that he judged a book by its cover and didn't even take the time to read the first few sentences before putting it back and starting a new book. Dedee bent over to put his other shoe on and stood up and walked to the door and stopped because he heard her crying badly. He opened the door and stopped, he did want to see her again, but at the moment he was mad and needed some time to himself. He looked a Coyia and said "I'm truly sorry for everything this ain't me I just need some time to myself right now, and I hope to see you around sometime," he started walking out the door and Coyia felted everything come out of her body all at once she felt, rage, hate, anger, jealousy and love and without thinking she turned over as fast as she could and grabbed the lamp and pull the plug from out the wall and ran at Dedee with full speed and yelled out loud saying "your mine and no one else's and she hit Dedee in the back of the head with the lamp and stood over him breathing hard and shocked. When Dedee fell to the floor Coyia stood over Dedee breathing heavily saying "nigga your to good to me and I swear before I let you walk out this door, you will love me and be in love with me or I promise you on that life want be the same for no one. Dedee looked up at Coyia from the ground and saw figures of her standing in front of him, the world started spinning and he passed out.

When Dedee woke up handcuffed to the bed. His feet was cuffed as well and his mouth was stuff with socks and duck taped covered his mouth. Dedee tried to scream but no one answered him. Coyia walked in the room minutes later because she heard Dedee yelling with the door open and said "no one will hear you and no one will even know that you were here. I already made sure of that so stop trying or keep trying if it makes you feel better. I already put sound proof windows on, and walls that are sound proof as well. So by all means keep trying if it makes you happy, o, yeah and sound proof doors that works wonders. I have been planning this for a long time, but never thought that I would actually do it until now. Dedee kept on trying to escape, but seen that she was right and stopped after a while. Coyia looked at Dedee and said "Im going to show you that I can love you and that I'm a great women, "Are you hungry", if you are please nod your head and let me know something, if not then fuck it, ill finish what I was doing"? Dedee just looked at Coyia with rage in his eyes and Coyia said "I'm going to clean your head up and fix your wound, so you're not sitting here bloody". "You are way to bomb to be sitting here with blood running down your face". Coyia walked out the room and went to the kitchen to grab a bowl and she put some dish soap inside of it and warm water. She went to her hallway closet and grabbed a face towel and wet it inside of her bathroom and walked back into the room to where Dedee was. She sat on the bed right next to him and started cleaning up his wounds Dedee wouldn't let her clean his head. Dedee had rage in his eyes and kept trying his best to move away from Coyia. Coyia laughed at him and said "Baby, stop moving, so I can clean you up please"? Dedee kept moving and Coyia started getting upset because Dedee wouldn't stop moving away from her, so Coyia got up and put her hands on her hips and said "Fine, since you want to be like that then, this is how we will play it".

Coyia walked into the hallway and grabbed a neck brace that she had worn when she had gotten raped from the hotel. She walked back into the room and grabbed Dedee's head and he fought her as much as he could, but couldn't do too much because he couldn't use his arms and his head could only do so much. She grabbed his head and forcefully put the brace on his head.

Dedee's eyes were bloodshot red and he was even madder because he couldn't spit on her after she put the brace on. So he just kept moving his head and Coyia stopped and stood up and looked Dedee in his eyes and said "I'm only going to say this one time and one time only, STOP MOVING YOUR MOTHAFUCKING HEAD SO I CAN CLEAN YOU THE FUCK UP"? Dedee just kept moving his head and Coyia bented down and said "Have it your way"? She grabbed a handful of dedee's balls and started squeezing them. Dedee yelled for dear life. He yelled through the sock in his mouth and said "Okay, okay", with tears in his eyes. Coyia smiled and sat back down and kissed Dedee on his bloody head and started crying with Dedee because she didn't want to hurt him and she said "Thank you baby for not moving, I knew that you would see it our way, i just wanted to help, that's all", and she took the brace back off. Dedee looked at her with confusion in his eyes. Coyia saw how he looked at her with tears in his eyes and she said "The only reason I said our way is because we are a couple and we do things as a team and there is no I in team". Coyia started cleaning Dedee's face in head. She bandaged him up and grabbed everything she used to clean him up with and walked towards the door and turned on the heat and the TV for Dedee. She looked at him with a smile on her face and said "I'm going to make us something to eat so you just stay right there in I'll be back baby." She blew him a kiss on the way out the door and went to the kitchen to cook them some food.

Coyia warmed up the food they had eaten the night before, mac n cheese, cornbread, cabbage with bacon in it and turkey necks and veggies. She walked into the room with two plates full of food and sat one plate on Dedee's chest and sat next to him after covering both of them with the cover. She took the duck tape off his mouth so he could eat. She started eating and watching the movie she had put on for him. She tried to feed Dedee, but he didn't let her take out the sock from his mouth. So she just left his food alone and started eating her own food while they watched TV together. When Coyia finished her food she put her plate on the dresser next to the bed and cuddled up next to Dedee after moving his plate to the dressers well. Coyia felt so happy having Mr. Right in her bed and she didn't plan on letting him go until he loves her. They watched TV and Coyia would look up at Dedee from time to time and kiss his face and tell him that she loved him and that she was glad they had put him in her life. She would lay back on his chest and hold him as tight as she could without hurting him. When the movie was over Coyia got up and asked Dedee one last time, "Baby, are you sure you're not going to eat your food before I go back into the kitchen"? Dedee didn't say anything or didn't make any sounds, he just looked at the TV thinking how to get free. Coyia grabbed the plates and started walking to the door and said "Oh yea I'm about to bathe you, I hope you don't mind, you remember what we did last night, shit it's getting my pussy wet just thinking about it now". She smiled and walked out of the room to the kitchen. Dedee looked all around the room for a way to get free but couldn't find anything in his reach. He tried to pull the handcuffs, but everytime he did they would pull the handcuffs that were hooked to his feet. Dedee thought to himself (smart bitch) and stopped after a while of trying to get free. Coyia walked in the room a few seconds later with a bowl of warm water and a bar of soap and some baby oil. She sat everything down and went to the dresser and grabbed her scissors and cut his clothes off his body until he was completely naked. She put the rags she had in the water and got it real soapy, then she started at his head and started scrubbing her way down towards his feet. She started getting lower and she noticed Dedee staring at her, Coyia smiled at him and looked at his dick and bent over and licked and kissed her new best friend.

Dedee threw his body at Coyia and she stood up and looked at him with her hands on her hips and said "My bad, I was trying to make your day, but I'll leave him alone, for now". Coyia started wiping the rest of his body with the soapy rag and when she got done, she oiled him down with baby oil and once again she got down to his dick and started playing with his dick. Dedee was angry and jerked and moved his body from side to side but everytime he did that he would cut his ankles or his wristed with the handcuffs. He just gave in and started cussing her out. "You faggot ass bitch, I swear when I get out of here ima kill you, bitch, you can try all you want to, but I ain't getting hard for yo ass"! Coyia looked down at his dick and seen that he was starting to get hard and she looked back at Dedee's face and said "I guess you in your dick don't think alike because he is standing straight the fuck up in attention, Dedee looked down at his dick that Coyia was rubbing and seen that she wasn't lying. He started moving from side to side and Coyia said "fuck it, we ain't going to let this go to waste," and she stopped playing with him and started taking her clothes off. She grabbed the baby oil and started rubbing her pussy down and climbed on top of Dedee. He tried his best not to let her on top of him, but all she did was put all of her body weight on top of him and with the baby oil he slid right inside of her. Coyia rode the shit outta of him. He was so mad that he couldn't throw her off of him so he did the only thing that he could do, he started spitting on her. He figures that she would have gotten up but she did the opposite and that turned her on, Coyia embraced him spitting on her and rubbed it into her skin, she even went faster and that just pissed Dedee off. He just laid there and let her finish. His spirit was broken because he couldn't defend himself.

Coyia squirted all over Dedee and asked him if he was ready to nut. Dedee didn't say anything he just laid there and Coyia told him that she was going to get one more nut then she would suck his dick until he nutted in her mouth. Coyia did actually what she said she was going to do. Dedee tried his best not to nut while she was sucking his dick but it felt to good and she knew what she was doing, Dedee tried to think of anything that would turn his stomach over or even upside down, but her head game was on point and he couldn't hold back any longer and he release himself all in her mouth, Coyia swallowed every bit of him. When he finished Coyia wiped him down once more and used the same water to wipe herself down then turned the lights out and put the cover over him and cuddled up next to him and fell fast to sleep. When Coyia woke up she looked at Dedee and saw that he was still asleep and went and washed her face and brushed her teeth and went to the kitchen to cook him breakfast. Dedee woke up to the smell of pancakes in the air and thought that he was dreaming, but when he couldn't move his hands or feet he realised that this shit was not a dream, in fact it was real life. He just cried silently to himself. Coyia came in 30 minutes later with breakfast in both of her hands and saw Dedee crying. He looked at Coyia and spit the sock out of his mouth and asked her "why was she doing this to him "? She sat their food down on the dresser and sat next to Dedee on the bed and replied "because I want to show you that I love you and that I can be that girl for you, the one you can call on and rely on". Deede looked at her with tears running down his face and said "By doing all of this to me, the man you're supposed to love, the one you are in Love with"? Coyia looks at Dedee and smiles, "don't say it like that this is the only way that I can show you that I love you, and want to love you only if you allow me to show you". While Coyia was talking to Dedee she was grabbing the baby oil and pulling the covers off of him and said "like now, I plan to ride you until you feel what I feel for you in this shorty time that we have met", we are meant to be together and I plan to keep it that way until otherwise". Coyia put the baby oil on Dedee dick and got on top of him and started kissing him and riding the shit out of him while she said repeatedly "I LOVE YOU", over and over again.

Dedee got mad and tried to get Coyia off him but wasn't able to, so he gave in but this time he started moaning. For some twisted way he always wanted a woman to take advantage of him, but not like this, how Coyia was doing him. For some strange way he moan and went along with it. After a while he snapped back into his reality after looking at Coyia's face. He started pulling his hips away from her and he bumped her off of him. Coyia foot hit the ground and she slapped the shit out of Dedee. He spit blood in her face. Coyia smiled and said "yes daddy, that's what I'm talking about daddy", and she rubbed the blood that hit her face all over herself and she climbed back on top of him. Dedee looked around in rage and seen the door open and he started screaming "Help, help!!!!!". Coyia covered his mouth with her hand and started to ride Dedee like he was a horse. Dedee bit the shit out of Coyia and she punched him in his head repeatedly. Coyia stood up and walked to her closet and grabbed a big ass leather belt and said in a anger voice "Mothafucka gon bit me nigga you must've lost your mind", she shut the room door and she started hitting Dedee across his naked body with the belt and she got back on top of him and put the belt around his neck and she choked him and rode Dedee until she came hard on him. Dedee laid there hurting, crying and in pain, he kept thinking to himself how was it possible for a man to get raped by a women. He laid there and let her have her way with him and he just cried. When Coyia had finished having her way with Dedee she laid down on his naked and sore body and apologised to him for losing her cool. She rubbed his chest hairs and fell asleep. Dedee laid there and thought about each in every way that he could escape but came up with nothing. He thought about his job and all the money he could have been making if he would have never met Coyia. He started crying and Coyia must have felt him crying because she woke up and asked him what was wrong, Dedee didn't answer he just looked away and Coyia couldn't help it but to cry with her man and to hold him until they both passed out.

Dedee woke up in the middle of the night because he had to use the bathroom. He tried to move up and down but couldn't wake Coyia up.

So he called out her name and she woke up, but went back to sleep. Dedee thought to himself that she must've been tried because she aint never not woke up and he started wiggling his body to wake her, but all she did was roll over. Dedee started sweating and he was starting to worry because he didn't want to piss on himself, he said" man, im to grown to be pissing on myself, fuck man". That's when something popped into his head and a light popped on inside himself. (Hey, if I piss on myself then she is going to have to undo my handcuffs so that she can change the shirts). He smiled and started pissing all over himself, then he looked at Coyia and turned as much as he could and pissed on her. Coyia started dreaming about having a water fight and she woke up to her body being pissed on. Coyia jumped up as Dedee was just finishing and said "what the fuck are you doing"! Dedee smiled and said "I tried to get you up, but you didnt wake up so he fuck it," Coyia didnt understood what he was saying but didnt like how he was smiling at her. She looked at his body and said "did you piss on me on purpose", Dedee started laughing hard and said "damn skippy I did bitch," that didn't sit right with Coyia so she shook her head and said "it's funny huh, okay, watch this". Coyia turned on the lights and looked around the floor for that belt she had beaten Dedee with earlier and said "I'll teach you about peeing on me bitch"! Dedee's face went from a smile to a frown in two seconds he started saying "I TRIED TO WAKE YOU UP, I TRIED TO WAKE YOU UP, PLEASE, DONT!" Coyia beat the shit out of Dedee, Coyia screamed "I bet it ain't funny now is it. She beat him like a slave," he screamed and agony and pleaded for her to stop, but she didn't.

Coyia hit Dedee everywhere there was skin on his body and all she thought about was being back in the hotel and how she woke up to being covered in sperm and urine from different man. The fucked up part about it was that he was pissey and wet everywhere, but Coyia was in her head and didn't see Dedee she just remembers how all the cold hearted men that she loved or had some type of feeling for has ever did her wrong. As Coyia

100

was swinging her belf she had hit the light and it had busted out, but that didn't stop her from hitting him.

Coyia hit Dedee harder when she busted out her light and it's like everything was a movie in the dark because she could see everything so vividly like she was actually there with those men again. Coyia swung harder and harder until she ran out of energy. She finally stop because she heard Dedee crying through the movie in her head and when she realised what she had did she screamed "O shit, baby, I'm sorry", she ran to turn on the lights but they didnt come on, so she ran back to the other side of the bed and turned on her lamp and she broke down and cried. "I'm so sorry baby", Dedee cried like a baby in pain. He was ass hole naked handcuffed to the bed by his feet and hands and had welts all over his body. Coyia sat there and tried to rub his body, but everytime she touched it, he jerked because of the pain he was in. Coyia looked at his dick and saw welts on it and his balls looked worse than his dick. She looked at his face and didn't know she was hitting his face and she cried hard and grabbed his face and kissed it over and over again saying "i'm so sorry baby". She really didn't mean to hurt him at all but she had memory problems that brought back flashbacks, bad ones and she couldn't control. The crazy thing was she was still somewhat sleeping, but really didn't mean to go so hard. His body looked real bad and Coyia hated herself she apologised over in over again while she kissed his wound like he was a little kids. Dedee cried harder than he ever did in his life, his mama's whoopins didn't have anything on this. He was being tortured by a crazy woman that wanted to show him how much she loved him. He thought(yea fucking right). Coyia started hitting herself and Dedee just cried and looked at her.

Coyia saw Dedee watching and went to him and begged for forgiveness. She begged like he was about to leave her for the rest of her life. Dedee just turned his head away from her and stared at the wall and cried to himself. Coyia cried harder because this wasn't what she imagined and things were starting to get out of hand. Coyia grabbed Dedee's chin and turned it to her and begged him to forgive her. She rubbed his body and then got up to get some cool water to help him out by pouring it on his body and blowing on it to ease the pain he was in. Coyia saw that Dedee started to chill out with his crying and Coyia told him her story about what happened to her. She told Dedee how she was raped by a lot of men that she never knew nor would she even know them if she had ever seen them in public. She told him how she was drugged and ejaculated and urinated on all over her and beat her pussy so badly that she was left for dead and couldn't use the bottom half of her body. Dedee had stopped crying and just listened to her and to be honest he felt bad but didn't know the story behind the sexy face.

This lady has been mistreated and raped and beaten to death. Even though he was chained up he just wanted to escape but now he felt for her even after that real life beating. It didn't change his mind though he still was going to kill her, but now he knew what to do and how to work the system to get himself free. After Coyia finished her story she walked into the hallway and grabbed a cover from the hallway closet and came back to the room and put it over Dedee and turned the lights out and told him that she will clean everything up tomorrow and walked out the room crying and grabbed a cover out the closet and went to the couch and cried herself to sleep once again.

When Coyia woke up the next morning she walked into the room to check on Dedee. She saw that he was asleep and that her room smelt like piss. She went into the bathroom and grabbed a bucket with soap water and some wash rags and dry towels. She sat those in the room and went and grabbed some clean sheets and covers from the hallway closet and sat them on the floor. Coyia pulled the cover off of Dedee and seeing how bad she did him and couldn't help herself she broke down and cried loudly. Dedee woke up and heard Coyia crying and holding onto his foot and he looked at her. She had her head down and she held onto his feet apologizing to him. Dedee didn't say anything to her, he just looked at her and turned back to the wall. Coyia walked around the bed to look him in his eyes and

Dedee turned his head once more and Coyia walked around the bed once more and said "please just let me say this to you so we can move on with our lives," he looked at her in said "What do you want from me, what"? Coyia looked Dedee in his eyes and said "please just let me show you that I can be that women for you and that I can love you more and harder than anyone one on this planet, please, if you let me show you this I will let you go, I promise, i'll take the chains off and let you go, so do we have a deal"?

Coyia held her hand close to Dedee and Dedee looked at his situation and really didn't have a choice, so he said "before I make this deal, I have my terms," Coyia said "I'm listening," Dedee said "no more fucking beatings," Coyia shook her head and put her right hand to the sky and promise that would never happen again. Dedee continued "No more chains, and you can't force me to love you back, or participate in anything without my consent, if so then I'm with it". Coyia looked at Dedee and said "The chains are staying on because I know once you get free I'm a dead woman, so just know I wasn't born yesterday, but i'll compromise with you and take one off everyday, because I see what it is doing to your skin and they look swelling up". Dedee said both of my feet today, Coyia looked at his feet and he responded. "It ain't like I can run, you still have my hands chain to something under the bed", Coyia said "Okay deal but, you can't fight me when it's time to put them back on deal"? Dedee thought about it and said "fuck it, deal!" Coyia said "okay, I'll take them off your feet, but if you try anything you'll meet my friend. Dedee shook his head and watched Coyia walk out the room and heard her going back with a set of keys that jingled loud enough to hear from another room. Coyia walked back into the room and grabbed her taser and made sure it was in reach. She took one of Dedee cuffs off his foot and then did the same thing to the other foot. Dedee let out a big sigh of relief and sat up and put both of his arms on the head broad of the bed and smiled because coyia kept her word. Dedee still couldn't get his hands free. Dedee looked at Coyia and told her to put on some music to better the mode of somewhat of freedom. Coyia smiled and grabbed the remote and started flipping through the channels until she got to some r&b music. {tony toni tone} {that's all I ask of you}.

Dedee started singing alone and said "cut the light out and make me feel better. I mean after all you did beat me half to death", with a smile on his face. Coyia looked at his face and saw him smiling and he whisper I apologise to coyia. "Coyia smiled and jumped up and down and said "o yea, I forgot I have a stripper pole in the other room, do you want me to go get it and set it up for you"? Dedee shook his head and Coyia and walked out the room to get the stripper pole from the other room and came back to her room and started putting the pole together as Dedee watched her. As Coyia put the stripper pole together Dedee said out loud "I better see you on that bitch with nothing on every night from this day forward, do I make myself clear"? With the biggest smile Coyia looked at Dedee and said "yes daddy".

When the pole was completely put together Coyia undressed slowly and put her red light in her lamp and started dancing slowly to the music she had played earlier and looked Dedee dead in his face to see if he liked what she was doing. Dedee's stomach started aching and he asked her to feed him and dance for him at the same time. Coyia did as she was told and even went farther and grabbed one of her diddo's and after she got done feeding Dedee she played with herself as she worked the pole as best as she could. Dedee told Coyia to walk to him because he wanted to taste her juices and she walked over to Dedee subjectively and sexy as she could be and put her pussy in Dedee face and he ate her pussy. Coyia really fell in love and saw that Dedee wasn't mad at her anymore and she thought about taking the handcuffs off, but he was doing great. He was chained up. Coyia squirted all over Dedee's face and it surprised her that he drank as much as he could while being chained up. Coyia fell in love at that moment once again. She moved the covers off Dedee and sat on his dick and made love to him. She went as slow as she could and made sure that she felt every inch of him inside of her. Coyia nutted almost a thousand times and got real nasty on Dedee and started sucking his dick then went down to his feet and sucked and licked every inch of his toes and toenails. Coyia made her way back to his dick and begged him to nut in her mouth. When Dedee finally came inside of her mouth. Coyia swallowed every bit of his baby's and lay down on his leg with his dick still in her mouth and passed out. Dedee was tired, but didnt fall right to sleep but for some reason this was the best sex he had ever had in his life. He always envisioned the women being tied up and him driving her crazy, but this was the best feeling he had ever experienced and he actually enjoyed it. Dedee started to pass out and Coyia woke up out of the blue and ran to the bathroom and slammed the door. Dedee jumped up and said "what the fuck is wrong with you", and he heard Coyia throwing up and he asked her if she was okay.

Coyia came back into the room and Dedee said "what happened", and Coyia just smiled and said "I ate too much when I was cooking for you", and she started laughing and apologizing. Dedee told Coyia to come to him and she crawled from the bottom of the bed and got to Dedee and he put his lips out and tried to kiss Coyia but she wasn't having it because she knew her breath stanked, but Dedee didnt care he said "Check this out, I'm naturally a freak, now come here"? Coyia smiled and said "you are so nasty, but I am too, but you're running the show". She got close to Dedee's mouth and he smelted what she was trying to tell him and he turned his head and said "Nevermind your breath does stank, baby go brush them real quick", and she pulled away from him and ran to the bathroom and brushed her teeth and put some mouthwash in her mouth. When she came back to Dedee she kissed him passionately and put the cover over them and Coyia held Dedee until they both went to sleep. As Coyia and Dedee slept peacefully as they could Coyia's cell phone rang and woke them up out of their sleep. Coyia reached and grabbed her phone and didn't recognize the number and forwarded the call.

When she got ready to cuddle back up with her man her phone rang again and she hurried up and grabbed the phone and answered it. "Hello, who is this and why are you calling my phone so late, the voice on the other end said "What's good baby, long time no talk", Coyia asked who it was and the man started laughing and said "this is your new man to be, baby, it's me the one in only E". Coyia's blood started to boil under her skin and her eye's turned red and she said in the lowest meanest voice that she could and said "Bitch ass nigga I have a man and I'm happy with what I have, now if you want me to give him the phone and have him chew you another ass hole for what you did to me and the other women I suggest that you don't ever call this phone in your life again ". For some reason that made Dedee feel real good because he always wanted a woman that went ham on her ex-boyfriend or any other man. On top of that she drove him crazy with that kinky shit she pulled. She gave him his fantasy in real life without even knowing what it was. Dedee looked at Coyia as she was putting the cover back over them and something snapped him back into reality and thought to himself "what the fuck him I thinking, this bitch got me chain up and I'm only acting like this until I get free or at least one hand free then im'a choke the life out this bitch". As he looked at Coyia with a smile on his face.

Coyia saw Dedee smiling and showed Dedee her phone and started deleting numbers from her old boyfriends and all the men she ever had in her phone. Dedee just smiled and wrapped his legs around Coyian tightly and rested his chin on her head and watched her finish what she was doing.

Days went by with the both of them getting to know each other. Dedee would tell Coyia some things about himself mixed with a lot of lies and Coyia just told him everything there was to know about her, plus more. She felt for Dedee really hard and knew that she could tell him anything and that he wouldn't judge her for her past and the men she had been with or the shit that men put her through in her life. Coyia was in love with this man that gave her everything just in a short amount of time and showed him as much as she could. Over time they did a lot in that room. They played board games and read books and watched a lot of TV shows and movies.

They would argue over movies and shows and laugh about it later. Coyia would fuck Dedee for days on in, because she loved how he sounded when she came all over him. Then there were those days where Coyia would just make love to Dedee. She would just slow grind on his dick and she would kiss him so sweet and long. She would kiss his body and lick his old wounds and suck on every part of his body that was visible. Coyia got really comfortable dancing for Dedee over time and started being more experimentable. She had found the bag she had the chains in and found all the toys in viberaters that they had never used. Coyia would put on nasty shows and sexy shows for her man, you know anything that she could do to spice up there sex life, she'd do. It seems like everything was good and damn sure getting better, at least for Coyia but Dedee loved Coyia when she got in a certain mode. He named it her love making mode. He named it this because whenever she got like this he could ask her for almost anything and she would give it to him. Coyia was sucking Dedee dick and he called her name "Coyia", she didn't stop suck his dick she just answered him "hmm", Dedee asked her to look at him and she kept on sucking and looked up at him and said "yes daddy", Dedee said "you should take off one of my handcuffs so I can play with you while you sucking daddy's dick"? Coyia stopped sucking his dick and sat up and looked at Dedee for a while. He looked at Coyia with a straight face in said "We know everything about each other and I feel the same way about you like you do about me, Besides, what can I do with one hand, you said you got mase and a Taser right, I just want to do more with you and really participate in everything with you". Coyia looked at Dedee crazy, because she knew he was right, but she didn't want to move too fast even though they were in that room for weeks with each other. Dedee broke her train of thought and said "come on, it ain't like i'm asking you to take off both cuffs, just one hand, you said you was only doing this until I let you show me that you could be that special women in my life, the women who wanted to show me that she could love me in every way possible right." "Will, I feel that way and like you wanted to say but I really didn't give you a chance to say, I prejudged you before I even got a chance to know you, the women I see now is not the women I knew a few weeks ago".

Coyia started crying because everything Dedee was saying was right in she knew he felt different even after all the hurtful things she had done to him, she felt that he forgave her and that she could take a small chance on one hand at least. Coyia shook her head in a yes movement and said "okay". She got up and walked into the kitchen and grabbed the keys to the hand cuffs and went to her purse and grabbed the Taser she had just in case things went wrong. When she got back in the room Dedee was looking at her and she said "Okay, check this out, if we do this and it works like I know it will, if we are still doing good in a day or two ill undo everything and set you free, do we have a deal"? Dedee smiled in a sexy charming way and said "deal". Coyia walked over to his left hand, as timid as she could be. All kinds of good feelings she was having about this new trust thing she was about to do but her head told her otherwise and something just didn't sit right with her head but heart felt great and ready for all of Dedee. When she got all the way to his hand she put the key in the hole and her head told her to look at his dick to see if it was at least ready to do something with her and it was limp. Her heart sank and she had a thousand questions go through her head and she let them out. Coyia stopped right before she unlocked the cuffs and asked Dedee ``Do you really love me Dedee, I mean really love me "?

Dedee shook his head and said "you know I love you baby, that's how we got to this moment, now come on baby take off these cuffs please, I'm trying to beat that pussy up and you keeping him limp baby"? Coyia asked "do you see yourself marrying me"? Yes, baby blood couldn't make us closer". Coyia planned on asking him a couple more questions and if he answers them correctly she plans on just taking the handcuffs off completely and seeing where it goes from there. "Do you want me"? Do you need me"? "Do you love me"? Dedee started getting frustrated because

Coyia was asking him way to many question and she was fucking up the mode. Dedee gripped his hand as tightly as he could cause he wanted to choke the shit out of Coyia because he felt like she was stalling on purpose and he just needed to get one hand free because the keys were in the room now and he could taste the fresh air from outside already, but he just wanted and needed one free hand. Dedee looked at Coyia and tried his best not to show his anger and he said "yes, yes, and yes baby to all your questions". Dedee forced himself to smile and said in his the comest voice "baby, now please can you let me out of these cuffs, please". Coyia had one last question and there was no right or wrong question, but she wanted to see what he would say, so she went for it "ask me to marry you then," Dedee snapped and went crazy.

"BITCH, I WOULD NEVER MARRY YOU EVEN IF YOU WERE THE LAST PERSON ON EARTH," and he brought his foot from the bottom of the bed and kicked Coyia as hard as he could. She fell back and hit her head on the wall. Coyia hit her head hard against the wall and she saw stars. Dedee was so enraged, he cursed her out like never before. "BITCH, FUCK YOU IN THAT PUNK ASS MARRIAGE, YOU HAD ME BUT NOW I KNOW THIS IS ALL FOR YOUR ENJOYMENT AND ENTERTAINMENT, I WAS SERIOUS ABOUT FUCKING THE SHIT OUTTA YOU BUT FUCK IT NOW, SHIT ALL THESE 21 QUESTIONS SHIT THROUGH ME THE FUCK OFF BITCH, YOU AIN'T WORTH SHIT YOU RAGGEDY SOULLESS NO HEART HAVING AS BITCH, FUCK YOU AND FEED YOU RAW FISH YOU NAPPY HEADED LONELY HAVING NO NIGGA BECAUSE ALL YOU DO IS FUCK ON EVERY NIGGA YOU MEET AS BITCH"! Coyia was rubbing the back of her head while Dedee yelled all kinds of hurtful things to her and he hit home on almost everything. That pissed her off and Coyia stopped rubbing her head and sat up slowly and stood up and looked at Dedee with the saddest eye's and said "I was going to cut you loose," Dedee cut her off "FUCK THAT SHIT BITCH, YOU WASN'T

GOING TO CUT NOBODY LOOSE SHIT, MISS ME WITH THAT BULLSHIT, YOU FAGGOT BITCH, IM DONE FUCKING WITH YOUR DUM AS BITCH, YOU ARE A DUM STUPID ASS BITCH WITH NO LIFE, JUST PLAIN ASS MISERABLE UGH"! Dedee spit a big ass spitwad at Coyia and it hit her smack in the middle of her face. Dedee yelled 'you like that shit bitch, as he kept on spitting at her saying "now rub that shit in, bitch"! He started throwing her past life in her face saying that what she got for being a hoe, and he wished those dude's would have killed her after all of them was done with her.

Coyia cried because she was really going to let him go, but after all of those hurtful things and spitting on her like she was nothing and throwing her past in her face and blaming her for it. Anger crept in and maddest turned into fury and hate. Coyia looked at Dedee and shook her head and said "okay, oookay", and started walking towards the door. As she got out of the room Dedee yelled to her "a bitch you promised you wouldn't beat me no more, you better remember what you said and don't go against your word, or was all that shit just a lie to, huh bitch"? Coyia didn't hear a word Dedee was saying she just grabbed her video recording camera and the stand that came with it and walked back to the room and sat it up right in front of the bed. Dedee just sat there and talked out loud and kept saying "bitch you said you wouldn't beat me again on my momma, I'll never forgive your scandalous ass tramp ass bitch, shit I knew my homeboys are looking for me and the police is to bitch, so fuck it, let me give them something to hear, aaaawwwwwww, aaaaawwwwww"? Coyia looked at Dedee and just started laughing and walked to the door and shut it slowly. Dedee started getting scared because he knew Coyia was mad, but how she laughed and jumped up in down made her seem like a crazy insane women and now he regretted everything he said about her or to her, he knew he shouldn't have spit on her or brought her past up but he was mad and anger. Now he knew she was about to hurt him really badly. Coyia grabbed a bag from under the bed and grabbed her Taser of the dresser.

She looked at Dedee and said "your right baby I promised you that I wouldn't beat you again and I'm a woman of my word". "See I have something else up my sleeve baby don't worry, im thinking and acting like a man, Bitch". Dedee started yelling at the top of his lungs "helppp MMMeee, please somebody help me"! He cried because of the unknown. Coyia smiled when she saw him crying and walked over to him and tazed the chain on the hand cuffs and he jerked all over the bed. When Coyia stopped tazing him he tried to say something "you stupid asss,"

Coyia tased his ass again. Dedee screamed in pain "aaaawwwww," and he begged her to stop. She tazed to chain again and he passed out. Coyia said out loud "o, no nigga, we aint done yet, I'm a stupid bum ass retarded ass bitch right, will ill show you one, bitch ass nigga"! She walked out the room and in to the kitchen to grab some hot sauce called spontaneous combustion and some canenye peppers a cup of hot water and ice cold water. When she got back to the room Dedee's mouth was wide open and Coyia walked right to it and put the hot sauce and the peppers in Dedee's mouth and she rubbed it all over his nuts and armpits. Coyia stood up and waited for the shit to work, but he didn't budge and that pissed Coyia off. Coyia grabbed the hot water and through it on Dedee's naked body. Dedee jumped back to life screaming "awww". Coyia screamed at Dedee "now, say sorry punk or this shit is going to get a whole lot worse for you".

Dedee said "fuck you, bitch", Coyia grabbed the tazer again and tazed Dedee's balls and he yelled for dear life, "aaaawwww, I'm sorry, I'm sorry, sorry sorry sssooorrrrrrrryyyyy, please stop"? Coyia stood over Dedee laughing hard until she looked at his nuts and seen how swollen they got and she ran to the bathroom and threw up. She walked back into the room and started laughing again until she saw his nut purple and blue and she threw up again, but this time she let it out all in Dedee's face. Coyia stood up holding her stomach and looked at Dedee in disgust and said "Oh, shoot, my bad I couldn't hold it any longer. Dedee was screaming because of the peppers and hot sauce on his armpit and genitals. On top of that his mouth burned and she tazed his balls. Something popped in Coyia's head that would be funny if I was pregnant and she laughed to herself and said out loud "don't I still have that pregnantice test in this drawer". She opened it and it was there she said to herself "i'll check to see later on when I have to pee".

Dedee was still in pain and his legs were crossed and he yelled and said "bitch when I get loose, I swear imma kill you in shit in piss on your grave".

He tried his best to pull his hands from the handcuffs, but it didn't work. Coyia just looked at him and said "you funny bitch, because when I get through with you, not one bitch in america will ever touch you again, say something now punk bitch". Coyia tazed him again on his leg and all he could do was scream in agony. Coyia pick up the bag that she had pulled out from under the bed and grabbed a long two sided diddo. Coyia smiled and said "I been wanting to use this with someone, hell, why not with you bitch". Dedee's eye's popped outside his head and he yelled as loud as he could "Somebody, please help me, please, HEEL PPPPP"!!! Coyia tazed Dedee once again and held it onto his skin until he passed out. Coyia then went and put his feet back in the cuffs and she poured hot sauce all over the diddo and poured the rest in side of his pee hole and she tried to put the pepper in there but it didn't stay inside and his hole was too small. So she poured the rest of the bottle of hot sauce in his eyes and went to the drawer to get the vassile. The cold water was sitting on the drawer and she threw the hot water on Dedee and the cup as well. He woke up in pain and cried for God help. Coyia saw some lube in the drawer and put in on the other side of the diddo and went and started the video recorder.

Coyia grabbed a handful of vassile and put some on herself and on Dedee's ass. He pleaded more than ever now and begged her not to do it "baby, please don't do this to me, please, I'm sorry and I didn't mean to say that hurtful stuff I was just mad because you didn't trust me like you said you did, please don't do this I swear I wont say nothing else bad to you and I will just love you please baby as he cried. Coyia had death in her eye's and just looked at Dedee and said "yea, I'm sorry", and she rammed the hot sauce side diddo in his ass as far as she could go inside of him. Dedee screamed, in agony in pain mixed with discomfort. Coyia kept pushing until it wouldn't go in anymore and she looked Dedee in his eyes and said "now you know how it feels to get rape bitch, the shit, I went through alone, now we have something in coomon". She put the vaseline on the other side and put it inside of her and she looked at dedee and said "now Watch you get fucked". The pain Dedee was in was hard to describe, Coyia acted like the devil. Flash back popped in her head from the men that did her wrong and she took it out on Dedee once again. "So you let your brother fuck me in the dark and made it seem like it was you, and yall laughed in my face like it was cool"! She pushed the diddo in harder. "You fucked me and just ran out the house like I was a nasty ass bitch with your weak ass three piece suit, you bitch made man"! She rammed it in a lot harder. "Now you had this chicken headed bitch sucking your dick while I ran to the store and stole all that shit to take care of you and I almost lost my life from speedy back to your ungrateful ass, bitch"! she rammed it and hit him in the face. Dedee's body wouldn't let him take anymore he passed out from the pain.

Coyia didn't hear Dedee yelling anymore and she looked up only to see him passed out. Coyia got up and looked for something to wake him up but could find anything, so she grabbed the cup on the fall that she threw at him and ran to the bathroom and filled it with hot water and came back to the room and said "your going to tell me that you'll marry me", I didn't do all this for nothing and she threw the water on him and Dedee up didn't wake up. Coyia grabbed the taser again and tased his nuts again lightly and said "tell me you're going to marry me or this shit will get ten times worse. Dedee woke up yelling "aaawwww". She tased him again "say you'll marry me or shit is going to get a lot worse"! Dedee yelled "I swear, i'll marry you, just please stop"! That pissed Coyia off because he made it seem like she asked him to marry her and she tased him again and told him to say it the right way"! Dedee said to Coyia with the rest of the little strength he had "will you marry me Coyia, please baby ", and he cried lightly from being so weak from the pain he was about to pass out again. Coyia didn't really hear him and tased him again and told him to make her believe it," Dedee cried and pleaded for Coyia to marry him and Coyia stop the abuse and said "yes, baby yes I will marry you", and she laid on Dedee and kissed his lips softly with a smile on her face and while the diddo was still in Dedee Coyia grabbed the other end and put it inside of her while she laid on top of Dedee and Coyia said "now with the confession from me I now pronounces us husband in wife and she played with the diddo for him in her and Dedee cried in pain while Coyia was in ecstasy. Dedee cried for the pain and because he knew he was going to die in this house chained to the bed because of other mens wrong doings and his angry and his stubborn ways.

Dedee prayed silently to God "Lord please help me, I don't want to die because of something I didn't do please, I need your help lord Jesus, please and please take away my sin lord in your holy mighty name I pray amen. Dedee looked Coyia in her eye's once more threw all the pain they were both in and said "Coyia, baby I'm sorry for what they did to you, I'm sorry for what I did to hurt you mentally, emotionally baby, I know I could never make it right or right the wrong that others has done to you, but if you can consider or even think about giving me another chance I promise you I'll be all the men you always wanted and needed. I'll be your light in the dark time and the food to your hunger, what I'm saying is, i would love to marry you"? Will you marry me for all the right reasons.? Can I Fix and rekindle what was broken? So will you marry me Coyia." Dedee forced a smile, threw all his pain his body was going through tears fell from his eyes. Coyia started crying and said" yes Dedee, yes I will marry you and she hugged him tightly. She had to pee and got up and grabbed the test and ran to the kitchen and grabbed a hammer and ran back to the room and said "baby, I forgive you but before we start that new life I need insurances so this is going to hurt you more than me and she hit Dedee's hand as hard as she could and broke his wrist. She ran to the other side of the bed and swung the hammer again and missed his hand because he wouldn't stay still so Coyia grabbed the Taser and taser him and broke his other wrist and both of his ankles. She kept tasing Dedee until he passed out.

Coyia started walking towards the door and looked at the camera and down at the pregnancy test again and at Dedee and said "why not". she stood over Dedee and pissed over his limp body onto the pregnancy test. When she finished she fanned the test off over his face and waited. It didn't show right away, so she put it on the dresser and pulled a suitcase from out the closet and got everything that was valuable to her in her house. Then she grabbed the chip out of the laptop and put it into her computer and sent everything to Nicky and told her not to watch this, just save it. Then she wrote a letter to herself and put the chip inside of the letter and walked outside and put the envelope in the mailbox and sent it to her grandmother's house. When Coyia came back inside she grabbed the pregnancy test and it showed that she was pregnant and Coyia was in shock. She was just playing, but didn't really think that she would be pregnant. Coyia cried hard because she knew there was no way in life that she could ever fix this with him.

This man that is in her bed handcuffed, raped, beaten and broken is her soon to be baby's father. She knew this could never be again, so she grabbed a pen and paper and wrote Dedee a letter of my deepest apologizing. She let him know that he was a soon to be father. She asks him in the letter to always keep his number so she could keep in touch with him on what the sex going to be. She went into her other room and grabbed Dedee stuff and texted his friend curty the address to where he was in before she sent the text she put her belongings in the car in then sent the text she put all his stuff on the bed he was chained to and kissed him and apologized one last time and walked out her house and left the door open so they knew where to find Dedee. Coyia got in the car in drove off crying and rubbing her stomach ready to start a new life with her new baby to be. She never looked back but hurt so bad because she knew she had to do it all alone . . . . .

Printed in the United States
by Baker & Taylor Publisher Services